BEND

GRAHAME CLAIRE

Bend (Bend & Break Duet, Book One) Grahame Claire

Copyright © 2021 Grahame Claire

All rights reserved. No part of this book can be reproduced in any form or by electronic or mechanical means including information storage and retrieval systems, without the express written permission of the author. The only exception is by a reviewer who may quote short excerpts in a review.

This is a work of fiction. Names, characters, places, and incidents either are the products of the author's imagination or are used fictitiously. Any resemblance to actual persons, living or dead, businesses, companies, events, or locales is entirely coincidental.

Editing And Proofreading:

Marion Archer, Marion Making Manuscripts

Karen Lawson and Janet Hitchcock, The Proof is in the Reading

Lori Sabin

Print ISBN: 978-1-951878-18-4

For those who bend without breaking.

PROLOGUE

"DO you take this woman to be your lawfully wedded wife?"
Neither of us looked at one another.
"I do."
There was no emotion. Certainly no love. Just a flat monotone statement. I felt guilty—desperate—and he no doubt felt a mixture of anger and confusion. And yet, he was here. With me.
The officiant turned to me. "Do you take this man to be your lawfully wedded husband?"
This shouldn't be my life. I should not be forced to do this . . .
The man had broken my heart and it had never properly healed.
"I . . ." The word *don't* passed quietly past my lips.
Surprise registered on his face, which morphed into anger.
"Are you playing with me, Beau?"
Shit. Shit. Shit. I couldn't do it.
But the alternative was unbearable.
"If we skip the rest, is it still legal?" My hands burned where they were connected to his massive ones. I couldn't stand it much longer.
The minister cleared his throat. "Well, no, I need . . . um, consent . . . to legalize the marriage. For you, Beau, to consent to this union. So, do you take this man to be your lawfully wedded husband?"

I hated that was what my life had become. "Um, fine. Yes, I do."

"Okay. I can now pronounce you husband and wife. You may kiss the bride."

He leaned forward.

I yanked my hands out of his and placed them on his chest. "Don't even think about it."

CHAPTER ONE

BEAU

"I HAVE NO INTEREST IN MARRIAGE."

"Then I sincerely hope you find some quickly." He leaned forward. "These nuptials are happening. You'll behave accordingly."

I liked—no, I loved—London. It had become my home. But my father's constant pressure to marry the man of his choosing had driven me to another country. Or at least it had forced me to stay there. But right now, I was arguing this ridiculous notion with a man I equally loved and loathed. No, that wasn't right. Today, I loathed him much more than loved.

"We aren't living in medieval times, Father. Arranged marriages died a few years ago." I pushed to my feet, finished with this conversation . . . again. "I have a closing to attend."

"The situation is of your own making. I gave you the chance to choose and you squandered it."

If there was one thing intolerable to Samuel Hollingsworth, it was arguing with him. I didn't do it often, but this was taking his power too far.

"Selecting a husband off a list of approved candidates isn't a choice."

His eyes glittered with something sinister at my defiance.

"Sit down. Alex Davenport and his family are here and delighted to get acquainted with you."

He didn't.

One look at his face and I realized he wasn't bluffing.

I had my limits, and my father constantly pushed them. I'd just discovered what I absolutely would not do.

Marry Alex Davenport.

I didn't know him. Had only heard of him because of his family's business reputation.

And I wouldn't marry anyone else for that matter either.

"You didn't force Lincoln or Teague into marriage." I hated to drag my older brothers into this, but I had to use whatever defense I could find. *I don't want to* didn't seem to be making the point.

His nostrils flared in annoyance. "You are my only daughter. I will not allow just any man to have you."

A chill skittered down my spine.

"I'm not an object." To him, I was. Nothing more than a robot to make him money.

He had the audacity to look angry. "Your hand in marriage is a coveted gift. By refusing to cooperate, you've put us in an undesirable position."

My father had put *me* in an undesirable position.

He'd stepped up the pressure, cornering me daily about this since I'd returned to New York.

"I have done everything you ask of me, but this"—I shook my head—"I will never do."

"I most certainly did not ask you to slum it with that—"

"It's done." I wouldn't think of Garrett Calhoun. And I wouldn't admit that my father was right. I never should've gotten involved with him.

That man didn't deserve my defense, yet I was offended by how my father had referenced him. But I wouldn't waste my breath taking up for him. Scum. That would've been a more accurate description.

He tilted his head and narrowed his gaze. "It better be."

Of course he knew what I'd been hiding. Not even my protective brothers had figured it out . . . and I lived with one of them.

"I'm going to be late." I stood taller, though I felt like a little girl in my father's presence.

"I've postponed your closing. You have no business purchasing that building anyway." He waved me off as if I wasn't capable of bringing in multi-million-dollar deals like I had for the past decade. He pressed the intercom on his phone. "Send in the Davenports."

Rage swirled from my toes all the way to the top of my head. There was only one other person who could garner this type of reaction from me.

I felt like a caged animal. Feral and ready to strike.

Except there was no escape. My father had won this round in a single knockout blow.

I gripped the back of my chair as Alexander Davenport the Third, according to the list of potential husbands I'd brushed off, led his parents into my father's office.

Father stood and pasted on a luminous smile that the rest of the world believed was the real him. "Alex, come in, my boy."

I was going to be sick. He'd never treated us that way except in front of others where perception was everything.

He bent and kissed Mrs. Davenport's cheek. "Della, you look lovely as ever." And then he shook the elder Davenport's hand. "Alexander. If this rain would let up, maybe we could get that golf game in."

They all laughed as if this were an afternoon of old friends, but we were at the office. Clearly, it was a business transaction.

And I was the commodity.

"This is my daughter, Beau." Father slipped an arm around my shoulders and squeezed.

I pasted on the same fake smile he wore. It was automatic after years of etiquette ingrained into my head.

I'm the prized cattle on display for purchase.

Mr. and Mrs. Davenport shook my hand with pleasant hellos.

Mr. Davenport gestured toward the younger man. "This is our son, Alex."

Alex stepped forward. "Beau. You're even lovelier than your father described." He kissed my cheek.

I stiffened, fighting down the bile threatening to surface.

"Hello, Alex."

Discreetly, Father pinched my shoulder. *Was my greeting not polite enough?* I'd have been more than happy to knee Alex in the crotch or shove my heel into his foot.

"We are thrilled about this alliance." Mrs. Davenport put her hands together in a soft clap.

"As am I," Alex said darkly.

If he thought he would get any closer to me than he was right now, he was sorely mistaken.

Play the game, Beau. Be smart.

I'd already lashed out to my father. He wasn't pleased. And if I wanted to get out of this mess, I needed to box up all my anger and use it when it was most advantageous.

Now wasn't that time.

"This union is such a natural fit. You and Alex are perfectly suited," Mr. Davenport said.

Because you want access to the power of Hollingsworth Properties.

Although I hadn't met them before, I was familiar with the Davenport family. They had their own successful contracting company, completing some of the most prestigious building projects around the globe.

But those with money always craved more. Their status was just shy of the Hollingsworth name. *What had they paid my father for the privilege of this alliance? How much was I being sold for?*

Because it most certainly came with a cost.

"They'll accomplish great things for our families."

I hadn't considered Alex was just a pawn in the game too. Though the way his gaze raked down my body, I had the impression it wasn't a hardship.

"Come. Sit. I believe this joyous occasion calls for champagne." Father ushered the Davenports to the sitting area of his cavernous office.

Alex gripped my elbow, holding me back. His gaze was greedy and triumphant. "In three weeks, you will belong to me."

I met his eyes but said nothing.

I didn't belong to anyone. Not him. Not my father.

Not to anyone but me.

And that would never change.

CHAPTER TWO

CAL

"BEERS. After our shift. You can't say no."

John Vigiano slammed his locker shut.

"Can't." I pulled my FDNY T-shirt over my head.

"Uh-uh. You've been saying that way too often lately. What's going on with you?"

Nothing I wanted to talk about.

"If I miss one more dinner at my ma's, she'll kick my ass." I put on a fresh shirt, a button-down so she wouldn't complain about how I was dressed.

"On a Tuesday? I'll never get you people with big families." He punched my shoulder. "What do I gotta do to get a beer with my best friend? Make an appointment a month in advance?"

I shrugged. Seemed that way these days. "Let's shoot for Thursday. I'll be coming off twenty-four straight and will need it."

He shot a finger gun at me. "I'm holding you to it."

I pulled out my phone and pretended to type. "I'm putting you in my calendar. Pencil."

He knocked my hand away from my phone. "While you're at it, you better put in ink Hollingsworth invited us all over to his place on Saturday."

"I don't know if I'll make it. Christina's on baby alert." I wanted a chance to hang out with the guys, but annoying the hell out of Beau made it too tempting to miss.

"How many nieces and nephews you got now? Do you even know all their names?"

"I just call all of them *kid*." I lifted my chin. "You heard about that promotion yet?"

We only had a few more years before they wanted us off the front line. After forty, a desk job or retirement were the options. I didn't like either.

"Not yet. Six people applied and I heard they were looking outside the department," he said in disgust. "You better think about what you're gonna do. You ain't getting no younger."

Not only did I love being a fireman, but I needed this job.

"I don't fit behind a desk." I grabbed my duffel bag and shut my locker.

"And that retirement won't cover your bills."

"Since when did you become a financial planner?" I fist-bumped him. "I gotta run. I'm already late."

"Tell Mama Calhoun I said hey. And maybe I could get an invite over for some good food sometime?"

There was a time when I'd have asked him to come now, but I couldn't. It was too volatile in the Calhoun household, and he didn't need to see that.

"Next time." It was a hollow promise, but it tamped my guilt down. "Hey, spot me twenty. I need gas but didn't have time to go by the ATM."

He pulled his wallet out of his back pocket. "Why would you when you got your ATM right here?"

He slapped the twenty-dollar bill in my palm.

"Thanks. I'll hit you back tomorrow."

"Bring me some leftovers and we'll call it even."

I shoved the bill in my pocket. "You know Ma's food is worth way more than that."

I hiked the bag on my shoulder, giving high-fives and fist-bumps to some of the other guys on the way out. My father's picture was the first and last thing I saw every time I came and went from the station. I was a sixth-generation fireman and had a trail of heroes behind me.

Miss you, old man.

I unlocked my '76 Suburban with the key and climbed in. She was old, but the first car I'd ever bought. I'd washed fire trucks at every station in the city until I had a down payment.

She fired right up, and I closed my eyes for a second. It had been a long day. Three fires, eight medical calls, and equipment checks in between.

My sister-in-law Christina *was* eight months pregnant, and the reason I couldn't skip this dinner was that my brother Joe found out the kid wasn't his.

They'd been together since high school. Joe had given her everything, even on a fireman's salary, but it wasn't enough to keep her from sleeping with his best friend.

Shit.

I was pissed off at Christina, but she'd been like a sister to me for two decades. Was I supposed to somehow love her through this disaster? I doubted I'd be able to hide my anger and disappointment. It had certainly solidified my own stance on marriage. It was not for me.

I hadn't talked to Joe about it yet. Ma said he was doing okay, but I'd have to see for myself. I popped my neck a few times. Then I'd decide what the rest of my brothers and I were going to do about it.

I threw my truck in drive and wheeled onto the busy street. The station was only ten minutes from Ma's house. I'd grown up in this neighborhood. In some ways, it was the same; in others, everything had changed.

I cranked up the radio and cracked the window. "Little Wing" by Jimi Hendrix blared from the speakers as I cruised down the familiar streets. I was born here, and I'd die here just like my dad and my grandfather and my great-grandfather had.

And if it was true that that bastard Lee Stanis knocked up my brother's wife, he was a dead man first.

I drummed the steering wheel. The Calhoun men weren't saints.

We'd all made our fair share of mistakes. Family came first. The department second. But we did not step out on relationships. Ever. Our father had instilled that in us from the time we could understand what it meant.

He'd worked holidays and crazy hours, but he'd always treated our mother with respect. With a reverence. The time they had together was sacred. He never left the house without telling her he loved her. And he'd brought home flowers every week just to show he cared. All my brothers who were married did the same for their wives.

I wheeled to a stop in front of Ma's house. The lights in the front window were on. I could make out my brothers Bobby and Aaron standing behind the sheer curtains in the living room.

Is it too much to ask for some peace?

In a family of six boys, yeah, it was impossible.

My hand was on the door handle when my phone chimed with a text alert. I grabbed it from the passenger seat.

Need you now.

Well, well, well. This was early.

I was tempted to blow off the family dinner I was dreading anyway, but I couldn't keep jumping to attention when I was summoned.

Little miss would have to wait. Family first. Always.

CHAPTER THREE

BEAU

"YOU'RE STARING at that phone like it might do a magic trick."

Teague pointed his spoon in my direction. Milk dripped into the bowl off the end.

I should turn the stupid thing off. Della Davenport had called me no less than six times *after* we'd spent an entire afternoon acquainting our families. As if my pending nuptials to her son were a marriage of soul mates instead of a business transaction.

I didn't give a damn about flowers or catering or the guest list. Because I wasn't going to walk down that aisle.

I shoved a spoonful of Lucky Charms in my mouth and chomped viciously.

"Annoying calls," I said once I swallowed.

"It's the craziest thing." Teague tipped the bowl up to his mouth and drank. *Dad would lose his mind if he saw that.* "They have this button. And you can turn it off." He touched his head with his fingertips and made a motion like his head was exploding.

I threw a piece of cereal at him. "Mine didn't come with that."

And why did I care what my father thought about how Teague ate his cereal? I couldn't even have dinner with my brother without our father invading my thoughts.

"What's he done now?" Teague's expression turned concerned.

"Just the usual. *What I say is law and you must obey,*" I said in a fake thundering voice. "Last I checked, I built a multi-billion-dollar European division. I'm pretty sure I don't need someone standing over me with a stick."

"Quit."

I slumped in my chair. "I know I shouldn't complain. Especially after what he did to you and Pepper." I sniffed bitterly. "Lincoln is like a shield between us anyway."

My older brother had kept most of our father's attention on himself so it wouldn't be on me. Unfortunately, he couldn't protect me from this.

"I meant quit the company. Get away from him. Start your own." He put on a begging face. "Preferably in New York."

Guilt niggled at me even as my defenses rose. Neither of my brothers had any problem expressing just how much they wanted me back in the city *permanently*. I appreciated that they loved me enough to want me around, but I'd needed to go to London to get out from underneath the shadows of the Hollingsworth men.

I'd missed my brothers though.

Every time I'd come to New York over the years, it became harder to leave. So I'd stopped.

I loved my life in London too. I'd made friends and found my little corner of the world. It was home.

Until I'd been summoned by my father to return.

I'd put him off for as long as I could manage. When he'd had enough, he'd threatened to take away my position. Maybe I should've let him, but I'd *earned* it. I wasn't going to let it go without a fight.

I'd been back in New York for several weeks and it was almost as if I'd never been gone. I hadn't realized how much I'd missed my brothers, even if they were overbearing. I'd made a family in London, but it wasn't the same.

"I don't want to quit." As hard as the role of vice president of the European division was, I loved it. Putting an ocean between me and my father had made it slightly easier to handle. But I loved searching out properties. Turning something in despair into something magnificent. Creating a portfolio of the most desirable properties in the world.

The business was exhilarating.

And I was great at it.

"I said start your own." He drained the rest of his milk.

"I don't want to do that." I spoke before I'd even considered the idea. But that was the truth. I liked where I was.

Once I figured out how to get out of this farce of a wedding, I'd be on track again.

You could just get on a plane back to London.

I could be there in a few hours. In time for breakfast with Lawson, Annie, and Joss. They were my close girlfriends and knew nothing of the hell that existed in New York. With them, it was like I had a different life. One that *I* chose.

I'd be safer if I went back.

But I wasn't ready to yet.

The professional piece of my life was nearly perfect. The personal . . . I had a lot to work on. Being around my brothers and my best friend had been good for my soul. I wasn't done recharging.

New York isn't good for you.

It was and it wasn't. I'd fallen right back into old habits as if I'd never left. But I was closer to my family than ever.

"I'm going to figure out a way to make you stay," he said with determination.

Dad's already beat you to that, big brother.

"Let me know what you come up with." I stretched and yawned. "Thanks for letting me come by for some late-night cereal."

"It's only eleven. And I was hungry anyway. You gave me an excuse to eat again." He swiped my empty bowl off the table and put it in the sink.

"I can do that."

He slung an arm around my shoulders. "Did you not hear? I'm working on convincing you to stay in New York."

I elbowed him in the side. "By waiting on me hand and foot?"

"It's better than shopping."

"And look what that shopping got you. You'd have never landed Pepper without me."

He kissed the top of my head. "Probably not. And if you're not around, who's going to make sure I keep her?"

I groaned. "Go to bed. Give her and Miss Adeline a kiss for me."

"I'll give you a ride back to Lincoln's."

"No."

Teague lifted a brow at my swift response.

I schooled my expression into something more casual and patted his stomach. "I'm good. I've kept you from Pepper long enough."

"She's out. Some of the ladies from Paths of Purpose came by today. It was good, but she's just exhausted."

I hugged him. "Give her the morning off." I bent and kissed Ash's nose. "You're so quiet, I almost forgot you were here."

He'd rescued the dog from a fire and she showed her gratitude by hardly leaving Teague's side.

"Talk to you tomorrow," he said as he held the front door open for me.

"Love you."

"Love you too. Be careful. And you could text me when you get home."

I groaned again and pulled on the door to close it. "See you later."

As I waited for the elevator, I checked my phone again. I had half a dozen messages, but none of them were the one I was waiting for. And that irritated me. Not that I expected him to jump at my every demand. After all, he worked just as hard as Teague did and was entitled to spend his free time as he liked. But I needed him. Which I partly hated. *Men.* Why were they all such pains in my ass?

Maybe I should've let Teague drive me home.

CHAPTER FOUR

CAL

"MA, for the love of everything holy, I don't want to talk about it."

Aaron smacked Joe in the back of the head. "Have some respect."

I leaned on the doorway to the kitchen. I'd walked into the house of chaos.

"I've been here an hour and it's like there's nothing else happening in the world. Christina got knocked up by Lee. The end." Joe shoved past me as he stormed from the kitchen.

I hadn't heard this place this quiet since Dad passed.

"I'll go talk to him," I said, following my brother to the front stoop.

He lit a cigarette and blew out a plume of smoke with an aggressive puff.

"Those things will kill you." I stood opposite him and propped my foot against the wall.

"Don't start." He was three years older than I was but had always acted like he was our parents' age.

"You think I'm going to stand by and watch you kill yourself and say nothing?"

He sank down to the steps. "Give it a rest, Cal."

"You wanna talk about Christina instead?" I sat next to him, resting my forearms on my knees.

"I'd prefer some silence, but good luck on that around here." He blew out another cloud of smoke.

"You need to come stay with me?"

He jerked his head in my direction. "She already left."

What a gut punch. I hurt for my brother. He'd been married over twenty years. Going home to an empty house, knowing she'd moved on when he hadn't even seen it coming? I felt for him.

"Maybe you need to get out of that house."

He dangled the cigarette from his fingers. "Maybe."

"What are you gonna do?"

He looked away. "What can I do? I couldn't give her what she wanted most so she finally went and got it somewhere else."

They'd been trying to have kids forever. Nothing had worked. Not even the expensive fertility treatments he'd had to take a side construction job just to pay for.

"There were other ways."

"She didn't want to adopt." He hung his head. "I thought a miracle had happened. That Dad was looking down and finally gave me a son."

I balled my fists. There was so much pain in Joe's voice it ripped me apart. He wasn't an easygoing kind of guy. He stood up for what was right and disarmed more arguments between our brothers than anyone else.

But he was a good man.

Had been good to his wife.

He didn't deserve this.

"We should've known way back when. Never used a rubber when we were kids." He snorted bitterly. "I just thought we were lucky."

He took another drag off the cigarette.

I couldn't fix this with my fists. Hell, I couldn't fix it at all. Even if the baby by some miracle did end up being Joe's, the damage was done. She'd been screwing around on him for who knew how long.

But I was going to pay a visit to Lee Stanis. He'd think twice before sticking his dick somewhere it didn't belong.

And I might talk to Christina too. She needed to face the damage she'd caused.

"Ma called her mother. Now the whole damn neighborhood is talking about it." He flicked the ashes. "I know she means well, but I don't want people in my business. I look like a fool."

"No. Christina and Lee are the fools." I folded my hands. "And people were gonna talk whether Ma does or not. She's just taking up for you."

He sighed. "I know. But all I want to do is forget."

I squeezed his shoulder. "It won't happen."

He stubbed out the cigarette. "You could at least lie to me to make me feel better."

"I've never been good at that." Except once. When it counted. Because that one lie was for the best.

He shoved to his feet. "We better go in. Ma will cry if we don't eat."

I followed him into the house.

"I don't understand why Sherry doesn't do something with that girl."

Joe's steps faltered at our mother's words.

"What's her mother gonna do? She's forty. It's not like they can make the baby disappear and things go back to normal." Bobby gripped his glass of tea.

"Don't you dare talk about making babies disappear in this house, Robert Calhoun." She pinched his cheek like he was six instead of forty-five.

"I can't do this."

Joe stopped moving so fast I ran into the back of him.

"You can. And you will. She means well." I gave him a gentle push.

She cupped my face when I entered the kitchen. "How's my baby boy?"

I kissed her forehead. "I'm good, Ma. Hungry."

She patted my cheek. "Of course you are. Sit. Sit."

She shooed us to the table. The chair creaked when my oldest brother, Bobby, sat. I took my place beside him at the old table. It had been my grandmother's. Too many meals had been eaten here to count. I wasn't much for arguing over wooden nickels, but I hoped one day this table belonged to me.

Though it probably should go to one of my other brothers. One of them with a bunch of kids and a family who could enjoy sitting around it every night.

"Where's Michelle?"

Bobby took a swig of water. "Taking the kids to dance or baseball or art. I can't keep up." He scrubbed his face as if *he* were exhausted from carting them around. "They're coming on Sunday."

"Sunday?"

"Ma's cooking a big thing for after mass."

Shit.

"I gotta work Sunday."

"Want me to talk to Dunn? If you tell Ma you're working one more time, she'll go down there and do it herself."

I didn't need my older brother or my mother talking to Captain on my behalf. I'd never hear the end of it from the guys at the station.

"I don't want you using your pull to give me special benefits."

He'd made Captain of his own station a couple years ago. I was proud of him. He'd had plenty of experience herding all of us, so some firemen were easy.

"Nina wants you to come to her dance recital." He rubbed his jaw again. "I'll have to check with Michelle about the date, but I think it's in a few weeks. It's her last one before she graduates."

I bumped shoulders with him. "Way to make me feel old."

It seemed like yesterday I was playing Barbie dolls with her and she could barely say an intelligible sentence. Now she was grown and getting ready to start a new chapter of her life.

"Have you seen my hair?" It was almost white now, sprinkled with a few stray black hairs. "If she tries to wear those cut-off shorts with her ass hanging out one more time, I'm gonna have a coronary."

His face turned an unhealthy red.

"She still dating that punk kid?"

He glared. "I'm gonna kill him. That's all there is to it."

I squeezed his shoulder. "I've got a good shovel."

I glanced around the table. Three of my brothers were missing. Obviously, Joe hadn't brought Christina, and Bobby had explained his brood's absence, but most of the time all the wives and kids came whether my brothers were here or not.

"Where is everybody?"

"In case you hadn't noticed, it's getting late." Bobby wadded up his napkin and threw it at me. "Kids gotta be in bed."

I snorted. "Please. It's all us old people who want to be in bed."

"Used to be for a different reason." He ducked when Ma set a platter of chicken cutlets in the center of the table in front of him. "Now I just want to sleep."

I avoided sleep like it was my job. If I didn't have the same dream every night, I'd try to do more of it. But it never failed. And the past few weeks, it had been worse.

Joe looked down at his plate.

"Sorry, man." Bobby had the decency to look apologetic. "I didn't think."

"Just because I'm not having sex doesn't mean the rest of you can't," he said dejectedly.

"When are you gonna bring a nice girl home for me to meet, Cal?" Ma scooped pasta onto all of our plates. Enough for three grown men.

"Yeah, *Cal*. When?" Aaron smirked.

It was unusual for the youngest, but I'd been named after my father at Ma's insistence. Pop was a humble guy. To him, having a son named after him was a big deal. He'd called me Cal from the second I was born and so did everyone else. I was proud I'd gotten my pop's name, even though I'd never live up to it.

I scratched my temple with my middle finger at my brother. "The only nice girl left is you, Ma."

Dinner rolls flew at my head from all directions.

"Boys!" She chided us but loved that we still acted like kids. If we were around her table, she was happy. "You can bring her to Sunday lunch."

I pushed the pasta around my plate. "I can't come. I gotta work."

She dropped her fork. "All any of you do is work. You're just like your father."

"Sorry, Ma. Tony asked me to switch shifts so he could go to his son's ball game."

She patted my hand. "You're a good boy, Cal."

Eyes rolled all around the table.

"Suck up," Bobby muttered under his breath.

"Did you say something, Robert?"

He cleared his throat. "That this is delicious. Don't tell Michelle, but she can't cook like you."

Ma beamed. "I won't mention it. And it's my job to take care of you boys."

"Can I get some leftovers for Vigiano? He was jealous when I told him I was coming over for dinner."

Her round face grew brighter. "I'll make John a plate. You should've brought him. It's been a while."

I couldn't. Because some of the excuses I'd used to get out of hanging with him were family dinners I hadn't gone to. I didn't need him coming around and mentioning that.

Then everybody would be mad. I hadn't spent time with my family or my friend in nearly a month.

Besides, tonight Joe didn't need the extra eyes.

"You need anything done around here? Mike said he fixed the sink upstairs."

My mother loved to take care of us but was slow to ask for repairs or things that were harder for her to do than before. Things my pop would've done.

She waved me off. "No. No. But thank you for asking."

It had always been loud around the table, even before my brothers had been married. I hadn't realized how much that noise was a comfort until it was quiet. I loved the laughter, the brotherly jabs, the stories that had been told at this table.

There wasn't a time I sat here that I didn't miss Pop. There was a hole that would never be filled. He'd been such a presence, and meals weren't the same without him. Nothing was.

But I was grateful Ma cared for us the way she did. Didn't matter how old we were, we could count on her.

And I could count on my family. Where would I be without them?

I rubbed my stomach and covered my empty plate with my hand when she tried to refill it. "Saving room for dessert." I rinsed my plate and set it in the sink, then wrapped my arms around Ma's neck from behind. I kissed her cheek. "Thank you for dinner."

"It's here every night if you want it." She pushed out of her chair. "Let me get you something to take to John. I made the Italian cake you like so much."

"I swear it's like you've been gone forever. She makes all your favorites," Bobby grumbled.

I grinned. "'Cause I'm the favorite." I took the boxes of food from her. It was enough to feed the entire fire station for a week. "Love you, Ma. See you soon." I kissed her cheek again. "You call me if you need anything."

"I will, baby boy."

I flicked my chin to my brothers and sent them a silent *call me*.

Loaded down, I piled all the food in the front seat of my truck. Before I cranked the engine, I stared at the unread text still on my screen. What did I think? If I didn't touch it, it would go away?

I dimmed the screen. Distance. We needed distance.

The SUV roared to life when I turned the ignition. I shifted her into gear but kept my foot on the brake.

That text.

It arrived early in the evening. What had sparked that? Usually they weren't so blatant.

Screw it.

I tapped out a response.

Meet me in twenty. You know where.

CHAPTER FIVE

BEAU

I TOSSED my earrings on the dresser.

They landed next to my phone, which lit with an incoming text. Almost midnight. I should be used to the mind games by now, yet somehow I hadn't learned how to school my emotions against them.

I read the words. Put my earrings back on and grabbed my coat.

Carefully, I pried the bedroom door open and looked up and down the hall. The coast was clear. I tiptoed over the hardwood floors. *Thank God I left my shoes in the foyer.*

I slipped one on and balanced on one leg to affix my other high heel.

"Where are you headed?"

I squealed and lost my balance, but caught myself before I landed on my ass.

"You should've been a ballerina," I said as I straightened and glared at my brother.

"It appears you're transitioning to a career as an escape artist." Lincoln arched a brow in that way only he could.

"For your information, I forgot something at the office. I was *trying* to be quiet so I didn't disturb Lexie or Eric." I threw my tote onto my shoulder.

"Not me?"

"You're nocturnal." I cocked my head. "Actually what's the term for *don't sleep*? A-sleep-tomatic?"

One corner of his mouth twitched. That wouldn't have happened before my best friend and her brother entered the picture. Maybe I should've introduced them sooner. I'm not sure either of them would've appreciated each other back then though. But I was beyond thrilled for them now. They were perfect together.

"I'll call Webster's and let them know you've created a new word," he said dryly.

I kissed his cheek. "It's called sleep. You should try it. Especially since you have a pretty lady in your bed now." I put my hand on the doorknob. "I'll see you in the morning."

"Beau?"

I was halfway in and halfway out of the apartment. Slowly, I turned.

"What is he doing to you?"

The *he* was no doubt our father. *You don't want to know, big brother. You do not want to know.*

I faked a bright smile. "Same ole, same ole."

Lincoln had been a protective barrier between my father and me all of my life. It was my turn to protect him. I needed to handle this one on my own.

He let out a dissatisfied grunt. "Don't forget you can talk to me. About anything."

Not this.

"Might I remind you of the same."

He pulled me in for a hug. Lincoln had never been afraid to show me brotherly affection, but sometimes he was so cold it caught me off guard. And in the moment, a hug was better than anything he could say or do.

I hugged him back hard. "Love you."

"Love you too." He made a grumble seem sweet.

I shoved him. "Go back to bed."

"Wait until morning to go to the office."

I checked my watch. After midnight. "Lucky me, it is morning."

I HOPPED in a taxi a few blocks from Lincoln's apartment building. I rattled off the address to Hollingsworth Properties, where I rode the elevator to the top floor, stopped by my office and crept down a few flights of stairs before catching the elevator again. There was no one around except a security guard, who half dozed and half looked at his phone.

Out the back I went, where I flagged down another taxi. Thank goodness this city never slept.

I switched cabs one more time before I pulled up to a hotel in Woodlawn. I'd been there so often the past few weeks that the front desk clerk discreetly gave me a key and the room number as I passed without incident.

There were only three floors to the hotel. It was old and worn down, but clean, and hardly ever crowded.

As the elevator car slowly creaked up, I clutched the strap of my tote a little more tightly.

What are you doing? This is stupid.

And it was. Beyond stupid. I was smarter than this. Better than this. But I had a plan. What was the harm in getting something out of this while I executed it?

I turned the key in the lock and slowly pressed the door handle. The room was pitch-black as I slipped inside and quietly closed the door.

My back hit the old wood and a solid body caged me against it. "You're late. And you know how I feel about waiting."

Like you ever cared about making me—

My thoughts screeched to a halt when his mouth slammed against my neck. It was rough, hungry, as if it had been weeks since he'd tasted me instead of days.

Instantly I melted at the feel of his hands on my hips. Strong. In command. Expert.

He knows what to do too well.

I squeezed my eyes closed to stop my brain. I didn't want to think. Only feel.

"For someone who needed me now, you took your sweet time," he growled against my ear.

Something about the way he spoke the words, the way I felt them as they covered me, made me feel only the way he could. No matter how I tried to make it stop.

"Would you believe traffic was a nightmare?" I asked breathlessly as I gripped his shoulders.

They were broad, solid muscle, and sturdy. Like they could be leaned on when I needed support. But they couldn't be.

He nipped the crook of my neck.

"Garrett." His name slipped out before I could stop it.

He pressed me harder into the door. "You know what it does to me when you say my name."

Because no one called him that but me.

I tilted my head back to give him better access to my neck. His lips moved in an impossible way. They feathered over my shoulder, yet branded me, hot and searing, with every touch. The contradiction was too much.

I ground my hips against him. His jeans and my thin dress did nothing to disguise the hard desire that pressed against me.

His body was so big, it dwarfed me. Gave me a false sense of protection. Because Garrett Calhoun was anything but safe.

I hated him.

For what he'd done to me all those years ago. For the effect he still had on me now. For taking up any space in my brain.

This . . . it was only physical. But I was so close to addicting him to these little trysts.

And this time, I wouldn't be the one left in pieces. He would be.

CHAPTER SIX

CAL

EVERY TIME I was with her, it was like a drive-by.

I got a hit of what I needed, then felt used when she immediately got dressed and left. The only thing missing was the money on the nightstand.

I should've put a stop to this weeks ago. Should've never sent that text that set this thing into motion.

We were old news no one had ever known about but the two of us. It wasn't going to work out then, and it sure as hell wouldn't now. Not even just sex.

But Beau, she wove some sort of spell on me that made it impossible for me to say no.

Or maybe I didn't want to. Maybe this was my chance to get another fill of her, one that would hold me over another eleven years.

The sun peeked through the curtains, casting a sliver of light on her dark hair as she put on her shoes.

"You gonna buy me breakfast?"

I regretted the question. It was meant to rile her up but made it sound like I was using her for her money. Everyone at the station knew the Hollingsworths were stacked, but Teague was so down-to-earth it was easy to forget he wasn't like the rest of us, struggling to get by.

Money had been a point of contention between Beau and me a long time ago. She wanted to do things I couldn't afford, and I didn't mean weekends in the Hamptons. Dinner, movies, bowling. She hadn't seen it as a big deal to pay, but it was to me.

"If I could stand to spend any more time with you, breakfast would most certainly not be on the agenda," she said without looking at me.

"Oh no?" I put a hand over my heart. "This is starting to feel a whole lot like you're using me."

I grinned, and she threw a pillow at me.

"Don't act like you're not getting anything out of this." She pushed off the bed and grabbed her purse.

Yeah, I was getting something. And I wasn't going to think about what it was.

I snagged her by the waist as she rounded the bed and pulled her between my legs. "Try not to *need* me until Thursday. I'm on twenty-four."

She shoved at my chest, but I didn't let her go.

"I don't need you."

My grin widened. "Funny thing. I got the text that says you do."

Her mouth rolled as she looked ready to spit fire. "Let me go."

I tugged her closer. "Is that really what you want?"

What are you doing, Cal? The sooner she's out of here, the better.

"What time Thursday?" she asked as if it pained her.

Why that question gave me satisfaction, I didn't know. But I liked that she was already planning to have me again. Maybe she needed this as much as I did.

"Seven."

"You have to be at work in an hour?" Her eyes rounded.

"P.M.," I corrected. "And like you aren't headed straight to the office."

"I have to shower first," she said coldly. As if she needed to get rid of all the evidence that I'd been inside her.

I released her so quickly, she swayed on her heels but didn't fall. That dig bothered me more than I wanted to admit.

She didn't react, not even a dirty look, and as the door closed behind her, that bothered me too.

I plowed a hand through my hair. Why was she in my bed? *Is that what you call this? Because it sure as hell looks like a low rent motel to me.*

I'd picked this place on purpose the first time, halfway in hopes that she'd take one look and run because it wasn't up to her standards. Instead, she'd walked in, ripped my shirt over my head, and taken what she wanted like she'd never forgotten what made me crazy.

Not even a *hey, what have you been doing for the past decade?* She'd sent a message she only wanted one thing. And that was fine by me because that was all I had to give.

She went back to her world, and I stayed in mine.

Except she'd stayed in New York longer than I'd anticipated. Beau should've been back in London by now. Hopefully whatever business deal had brought her here would be done soon. I couldn't keep this up.

It wasn't just because it was a no-strings hookup necessarily, because what man wouldn't want that? Beau was hot. A goddess in bed. It was how cold she was afterward . . . how much distance she obviously wanted between us. As if she despised me. That stung. People didn't hate me. Except Beau Hollingsworth.

I swiped my keys off the nightstand. *I have to get out of here.*

Her scent still lingered. She was gone, but I could feel her nails digging into my back like she'd never left. The rumpled sheets hanging halfway off the mattress were a further reminder of just what a mistake it was.

But I wouldn't delude myself.

I'd keep this up until she went back across the ocean. I could make it that long.

You should put a stop to this. Now.

A gold earring glinting against the white sheets caught my eye. I grabbed it and stared at it in my palm. I wasn't stopping anything.

I checked my reflection before I left the room.

You're an idiot. You think you can do this and go back to life as usual?

Didn't matter what I thought. I had to. Because a woman like Beau didn't belong to men like me.

I slid the key across the front desk.

The clerk tapped on her computer and frowned. "Mr. Calhoun, I'm sorry but this form of payment isn't going through."

Shit. I was maxed out again.

"Someone stole my account, and I'm still getting it straightened out." The lie rolled off my tongue so easily because I'd said it a thousand times before. I pulled my wallet from my back pocket. The only cash was the twenty Vigiano had given me.

I gave her my debit card and prayed that there was enough in the account to cover the bill as she swiped it through the machine.

After a few seconds, she smiled and returned the card. "You're all set. See you soon."

I didn't get paid until next week. This twenty was all I had to hold me over until then.

Damn it. Again. Get it together, Cal.

If Beau wanted me again on Thursday, I'd have to do something I swore I wouldn't when this whole thing started.

Take her to my house.

CHAPTER SEVEN

BEAU

"I'M glad to see you've warmed to this union."

Father sauntered into my office and made himself at home in a chair across from my desk.

"Della Davenport said you had the loveliest lunch."

I'd tried to politely decline, and then not so politely, but she'd been like a bulldog with a bone, insisting we had so little time.

So I'd sat through two hours of her planning a wedding that wasn't going to happen. What had possessed me to pretend to care was beyond me. Maybe it was self-preservation kicking in.

I hadn't figured out how I was going to get out of marrying Alex, but my instincts were to play along as if all were well. My head wanted to tell my instincts to take a hike.

"She's quite enthusiastic about it," I said, setting the pen in my hand on the desk.

Father's gaze narrowed. "Do not get any foolish ideas, my dear. Remember I know what you're thinking before you do. You've fought me on this for a long time." He leaned back. "I don't believe you'll simply do as you're told now. Not for one second."

He was onto me. Maybe I'd have been better off if I'd told her if she wanted this wedding so bad to plan it herself.

But I had to come up with something to throw my father off. *Good luck on that.* He seemed to have this sixth sense about everything.

"I don't want to marry Alex." Just thinking about the way he leered at me made my skin crawl. Made me want to run to Cal. And that was completely bizarre. I did not need men like Cal in my life. "But I understand the importance of the arrangement. I just need some time to get used to it."

Did that sound convincing? It felt a little off, but hopefully it was enough to placate him.

He studied me with that gaze that I swore had a beeline straight into my head. Meanwhile, I had no idea what my father was thinking . . . other than something else to make my life miserable.

"You haven't offered a replacement for your position overseas."

I hesitated, carefully considering my words. "This is a marriage of appearances. No one would expect a transition to a new executive to take place overnight. I'll continue on until we find someone up to our standards."

"You cannot avoid his bed forever. Children are expected."

Ugh. My stomach turned over at the thought of allowing that man to touch me, let alone bringing innocent children into an environment where there was no love. I wasn't exactly the mothering type, but I refused to pass off children to a nanny and see them only on holidays.

"And European culture and history would be excellent for them to flourish."

Why was I even entertaining him about children who didn't exist and never would?

"I don't disagree, but they will be raised here. Under my influence."

What would be worse? Alex or my father?

I didn't think Alex was as ruthless and cold as Samuel Hollingsworth. No one was.

"I expect you'll find a suitable property to reside in."

Oh, I was thinking of living with Lincoln forever.

"Do you have any thoughts, Daddy? It's short notice and are we sure the Davenports have the cash to make that kind of purchase so quickly?"

I hated using any sort of endearment toward my father, but I'd learned at a young age that something about it softened him . . . a little.

"I do. We'll view them in the morning." For a moment, his tone was that of a loving father helping his daughter find the home of her dreams. He pushed out of the chair. "You have a date with Alex this evening."

No. I had a date with Eric for a piano lesson. He'd be so disappointed if I let him down.

"I hope he proves he's worthy. I'm sure a lot of people would be very eager to take his place." And I had to find one of them like *now*.

"That's right, my dear. I won't give you to just anyone."

You already are.

But I gave him a tight smile before he disappeared. *Go away and never come back unless you want to be a real father.*

I slumped. Teague and Lincoln rarely talked about our mother. I'd been too young when she passed away to truly know her. But they'd said how free-spirited and loving she was. I never could mesh that in my head with who my father was. Nor how she would have loved someone like him, when I wanted someone so very opposite of him.

Would he have been better if she'd lived?

Would I?

I'd been raised by three men. Four if I counted Winston, who I most certainly did. I hadn't had a woman's influence. I'd gotten my sense of style from magazines and watching the ladies in our circle of people. I'd learned to carry myself by mimicking runway models and Father and my brothers.

I'd done a decent job of appearing feminine, though I lacked the confidence to be certain I'd pulled it off. If Mom would have been around, would I have been more like her instead of my father?

My phone buzzed on the pile of papers littering my desk.

I grinned as I answered the phone. "I'm afraid I'm not available for dinner and dancing this evening."

"A tragedy if I've ever heard one." Cagan Roqueford sighed into the phone. "I've just arrived in New York and was hoping to get a tour."

"Are you buying the drinks?" I snatched my purse off the floor.

"If I must," he said dryly. "Where shall I meet you?"

"A bar." I closed the door to my office behind me.

"I'm here for business, not a social visit." A series of car horns blared in the background. "Must I ask the driver for a recommendation?"

"Park and East 33rd." I was tempted to ask him to pick me up, but I needed to get out of this building. "And you asked me for a tour, so I'm not sure I believe this isn't a social trip. Are Bennett, Annie, Lawson, and Joss with you?"

"Afraid I left them in London."

"Like you didn't have room for them in that massive jet." I pushed out into the spring warmth. People and cars swirled around in a chaos that somehow made perfect sense.

"It's just a quick pop over and back."

I smiled as I hailed a taxi. "Then I feel so special you called."

I WAITED on the corner of Park and East 33rd. The line at the food truck was steady but moved quickly. I'd heard good things about it, especially the cake. An afternoon pick-me-up to get me through the hellacious evening that awaited me was exactly what I needed.

A dark Range Rover stopped at the curve. Long legs clad in a custom-tailored pinstriped suit appeared first. Cagan stepped out of the back as if this city belonged to him. In so many ways, he reminded me of Lincoln. Could have been the suits, though Cagan preferred three-piece, but mostly it was their general air-of-command. He headed his father's global shipping company from London. We'd met at local council meeting when we were both attempting to get properties approved for rezoning.

Cagan Roqueford was a good-looking bastard. The kind who was far too handsome for his own good. We'd become fast friends, mostly because we liked to talk business. It was a shame he'd never made my heart beat a little faster or my skin tingle.

But that part of me was broken.

He made quick strides to reach me, bending to kiss both of my cheeks. "Hello, love. I hate to admit it, but America suits you."

I held him at arm's length. "I hate to admit it, but I'm glad to see you."

His grin was cheeky. "I'm not surprised."

I tucked my arm into his. "How do you feel about cake instead of coffee?"

He eyed the food truck warily. "Bizarrely better."

We filed to the back of the line. "What brings you over?"

"One of our ports had a software crash." He rubbed his temples. "It's a bloody nightmare. My father seems to think I'm an IT expert all of a sudden."

I bit my lip to keep from laughing. "Shouldn't you be headed to the port?"

"Absolutely, but the flight over wasn't enough time to steel myself for what awaits me there." He lifted a brow. "Believe it or not, I'm procrastinating."

"I don't believe it." We'd been friends for over ten years. He took the word workaholic to a new level and certainly wasn't afraid to tackle problems head-on.

We stepped up to the window.

"Good afternoon. What can I get you two?" a polite woman greeted with a radiant smile.

"We're here for the desserts," I said.

"Then I have just the thing for you . . . *if* you're feeling adventurous." She pointed to a display. "We have cake pops for the first time. Red velvet, birthday cake, and carrot."

"We'll take two of each," Cagan said, pulling out his wallet.

I gaped at him. "You really are procrastinating. Or planning to pass out in a sugar coma until the computer system is back up."

"Both." He stuffed the change into the tip jar.

"Enjoy." The woman handed us a paper bag which I greedily took.

"Are you up for a stroll in those shoes?"

I cut my eyes over to him. "I sleep in heels."

He snickered. "Very well then." He reached for the bag and I held it out of his grasp.

"What's your poison?"

"I'll have a red velvet, please."

I unwrapped the dessert on a stick and passed it to him. "Good, because I'm going with birthday cake. I don't know why you bothered with carrot." I wrinkled my nose.

We wandered for a few minutes, snacking and walking through the throngs of people on the sidewalk.

"Out with it," he said. "You're skipping work and eating sugar. I've never known you to do either." He paused to level me with a look.

It was true. I didn't do either very often. *Lately, you've been putting off a whole lot of work to run to that motel.* My heart rate picked up and my skin got tingly just thinking about Cal's big body against mine.

So that part of me wasn't completely broken. I just reacted to him. No one else.

I licked a piece of icing off the stick. "Undue stress."

"Wrong. You always have that."

"Would you consider marrying me in the next week?"

He choked on the bite of cake he'd just taken. "I beg your pardon?"

"Is it that horrible a thought?" I feigned offense at his reaction.

He cleared his throat a couple of times. "No. No. Just a bit of a shock."

"It could be perfect," I said, warming to the thought. "We're friends. Our families are from the same echelon. And you aren't so bad to look at." My father would be furious if I skipped out on Alex, but the Roqueford name had all the prestige he was looking for. In fact, they were *more* important than the Davenports. And as far as business, it might be a good diversification for both families.

He tossed his empty stick in a nearby trash bin. "As tempting as your offer is"—he shook his head a little as if in disbelief—"and incredibly uncanny in timing, I can't accept your proposal."

Dang it.

"Not even to help out an old friend?" I asked extra sweetly. "We could get a divorce in a few years if you like." My father would have a fit over that, but it was a risk I was willing to take if it kept me away from Alex Davenport.

"What's brought this on?"

I sat down on a bench. "My father arranged a marriage for me."

Cagan's lips parted. "Bloody hell. That's . . . unfortunate." He touched my knee. "I take it you don't care for the bloke."

That was putting it politely. I hadn't really given Alex a chance, but I went with my instincts. And they didn't care for him one bit.

"No."

"And these nuptials are when?"

"Three weeks . . . twenty days if you want to be specific." I looked up at the sky. "Should I send you an invitation?"

"Do you need me to be there?"

I snapped my head toward him. Genuine concern stared back at me.

And for a moment, I smiled. This was what I'd been missing since being in New York. I could be me with Cagan. Genuine. Honest. How I'd missed my friends.

"No," I finally said. "Will you think about helping me? Please." I was begging, but if it got me out of marrying Alex, I'd do it forever.

His eyes softened with apology. "Beau, I—"

"Don't say no yet," I said quickly. "Get your shipping port running again, then consider it on the flight home. Think about what you want in return."

"Beau . . ." he said warily.

"Please."

He sighed. "I'll think about it. But I'm not promising anything."

I threw my arms around him. "Thank you."

Relief that I just might get out of this raced through me.

"No promises," he said more firmly.

"How about to keep this between us?" My elation was out of control. He hadn't said yes, but I felt as if he had.

"That I can do."

CHAPTER EIGHT

CAL

"FIRST ROUND IS ON YOU."

Vigiano slapped my shoulder with a grin.

Damn. In the frenzy of the past two days, I'd forgotten my promise to hang out. We'd spent all day putting out a monster of a blaze, and I just wanted to go home.

And text Beau.

No. I did *not* need to be doing anything stupid like that. Beers with Vigiano was the perfect solution.

"Scopetta and Brennan are coming too."

"I'm not paying for their sorry asses." I toweled off my chest, the idea of going to the bar growing on me.

I hadn't seen my friends much outside of work. Sometimes I had more than enough of them there. Maybe I'd have something stronger than beer so I'd go home and pass out. *And not invite Beau over.* Because I had to cut this thing off.

You should've never let it go on this long.

I shouldn't have started it in the first place. But when I'd seen her again at Cassano's funeral, that fire of hate in her eyes when she looked at me, I wanted to tame that blaze. Turn it into something else.

Vigiano pulled on a T-shirt. "Hell of a day, wasn't it?"

"Crazy." I rifled through my bag for a pair of clean jeans.

"You've been quiet lately."

And I didn't feel like being called out on it now.

"Had a lot on my mind." Family pressure. Money pressure. Work pressure. *Beau.*

"Which is why we need the beers so you can unload it."

I looked at him in disgust. "It's beers. Not therapy." The point of the drinks was to forget all of it, not wallow in it.

He laughed. "Hurry up and get dressed, pretty boy. Let's get out of here."

DONNOVAN'S WAS FILLED with the after-work crowd who had stayed for a few too many drinks.

"Hey!" Brennan waved us over to a table they'd grabbed near the bar.

"I'll get a round," I grunted as Vigiano forked off toward our friends.

"Cal, where you been hiding?" Roy Donnovan slapped my hand when I leaned against the bar.

"Here and there."

He popped the top on four beers and slid them over the surface. "Quinn came in asking for you the other day."

My grasp on one of the cold bottles slipped, but discreetly I readjusted my hold. "Thanks." I held up a beer in salute.

Of course. *When it rains . . .*

"I'll put these on your tab."

I nodded and made my way across the bar.

"Thanks, honey," Scopetta said when I deposited the drinks on the table.

I gave a little curtsey and pretended to fluff my non-existent shoulder-length hair.

"He's the ugliest waitress I ever seen." Brennan threw a peanut at me.

"You been eating those?" I pointed to the bowl as I turned my chair backward and sat.

The grin fell from his face. "Yeah. Why?"

I took a sip of my beer. *Damn that was good.* "No reason."

"What's wrong with the peanuts?" Brennan looked at the other guys with lines creasing his forehead. "Why am I the only one eating them?"

Scopetta groaned. "Look what you started, asshole."

I picked up a nut, tossed it in the air, and caught it with my mouth. "Happy now?"

He settled back into his chair. "A little."

"Cal, you keep shit stirred up," Scopetta said, taking a swig of beer.

Wasn't that the truth?

"I heard a rumor about Christina and Stanis."

Any tension that swallow of beer had released came back tenfold. "And you better keep that rumor to yourself."

Vigiano twisted toward me, brow furrowed. "What's he talking about?"

"Garbage," I said, trying to cut this conversation off at its knees.

"Don't sound like it," he pressed.

I flashed him a look to let it go. "Well, it is."

An uncomfortable silence came over the table. My already sour mood had taken a nose dive. To believe Joe was finally getting the baby he'd hoped for, yearned for, for years, only to find out the kid wasn't his would be awful. It was a shit thing Christina did to Joe in the first place, but to wait until nearly the due date to tell him? I didn't know what that did to a man. But I wouldn't allow his buddies here to make it a point of gossip. My brother deserved more than that.

"Your grandmother okay?" I asked, flicking my chin at Scopetta.

"Mad as hell she's in the rehab instead of at home." He spun his beer on the table. "Stubborn woman needs to move in with my parents or Aunt Luna, but she says a broken hip won't stop her."

"She could move in with you." I smirked.

Another peanut sailed in my direction. "My love life sucks as it is. I'd never get laid if she lived with me."

"You never get laid anyway." Vigiano pointed out.

"Like you do either."

Here we go. They'd argue the rest of the night about who slept with more women. Sometimes it was funny, but tonight I was in no mood. It was my fault since I'd started it.

The front door to the bar burst open. "Joe's beating the shit out of Lee Stanis!"

I jumped from the table and sprinted outside. Joe had Lee in a headlock, landing blow after blow to his face.

Pull him off, Cal.

I would. But I wanted my brother to have some form of justice, even if it was short-lived.

Lee threw his arms around wildly, landing a few punches on my brother's ribs and legs and back. Joe didn't seem to feel them. Like a robot, he just kept hitting him in the same place.

When Lee stopped moving, I stepped forward. But Joe let go of him. He dropped to the ground in a heap.

My brother stood over his best friend, chest heaving. "Thirty years of friendship. You do this to me. You're lucky I don't kill ya."

I clamped a hand on Joe's shoulder. "Let's get out of here."

Anybody else, I would've made sure he was breathing, but that scumbag . . . somebody else could do it.

I flicked my chin at Vigiano who nodded back. Joe let me steer him to my truck as if he were on autopilot. He climbed in the passenger side, and I shut the door.

"I was gonna take care of him," I said as I cranked the engine. Tonight, I'd been planning to pay him a visit.

"Ain't your job to take care of it." Joe stared out the window.

"What if they suspend you? Then what?" I wheeled into the street and turned at the next block.

"I can't go back there."

We weren't far from his house. I'd assumed he'd want to go home.

He hung his head. "They were screwing around in my bed." His voice was lethally quiet. "She told me that today."

Oh no.

What was the matter with Christina? Was she trying to intentionally kill my brother? Lee Stanis wasn't the only one I needed to have a word with. My soon-to-be ex-sister-in-law was on that list.

"I told you you can come stay with me."

"You got a life—"

"And I'm at the station most of it." I pulled over in front of his house. "What do you need? I'll go in and grab it."

He shrugged.

I jogged up the front steps to the brownstone and inserted my key in the lock. Maybe my family was weird, or maybe just invasive, but we all had keys to each other's places.

The house was dark when I stepped inside. I fumbled along the wall for the light switch and blinked a few times when the foyer light came on.

I climbed the stairs to his bedroom and looked around. Bed was unmade. An empty whiskey bottle was turned over on the nightstand. But everything else was tidy. Joe had always been like that.

I opened the closet and grabbed a duffel bag from the top shelf. Thank God my brother was neat. I pulled shirts and pants off the hangers and shoved them into the bag. One of his department button-downs caught my eye and I snatched a couple of those too.

I rifled through his drawers for socks and underwear. It was hard enough packing for myself, let alone trying to figure out what he'd want for a few days.

I'd come back when he was up to telling me what he needed.

Toothbrush.

I stuffed his shave bag with what bathroom crap I could find and dumped it in the duffel too.

I skidded to a stop halfway down the stairs when I found Joe standing in the foyer, door wide open behind him.

He lifted his gaze to mine. "Wanna help me burn this place to the ground?"

CHAPTER NINE

BEAU

"WE'LL HONEYMOON IN ST. TROPEZ—"

"I don't have time for a honeymoon." I flashed Alex the most unapologetic apologetic smile ever given in the history of smiles. I placed my napkin on the table. "And I have to go. With all this wedding planning, I'm incredibly behind on work."

I pushed back from the table.

He clamped a hand on mine. "We're not finished, sweetheart."

I looked down at where he was not so gently holding me in place. *We never got started... sweetheart.*

"Thank you for dinner." I forced the words out in a detached pleasant tone as I lifted my hand.

He held it in place, squeezing harder. Pain radiated from my pinkie. It wasn't broken, but there would most definitely be a bruise.

"Kindly take your hands off me." Years of refinement had taught me how to maintain control when speaking. I didn't want to draw attention to myself because I was humiliated I'd let this farce go this far. And now I'd have the injuries as a big fat *I told you so* to taunt me.

"Sit down."

Honestly, I wouldn't have thought Alex had this in him. I hoped this wasn't a preview of what was to come for whoever he did marry.

"Might I remind you what's at stake? I can't imagine your parents will be too pleased if this wedding doesn't happen."

He squeezed harder and I bit back the cry of pain that threatened to escape.

"The wedding is happening."

"If my father finds out that you've treated me with anything less than perfection, I assure you it won't." A little lie never hurt. To the outside world, he was a doting father, so the fib was believable.

His eyes narrowed into uncertain slits. "He isn't going to find out, is he?"

He had no idea what he was "marrying" into.

"My father is everywhere."

And that was an absolute truth.

He glanced around nervously but squeezed to the point I thought my fingers were going to snap. "When you belong to me, I expect more compliance."

"I'm sure you do."

I picked up my fork and stabbed the top of his hand.

"Shit!" he cried, immediately releasing me.

The entire restaurant looked in our direction. I discreetly set the fork in place, smiling to myself at the four dots of blood pooling on the top of his hand, collected my purse, and exited with my head held high.

My hand throbbed with excruciating pain. If that bastard broke my fingers, that fork would be the least of Alex's worries. I didn't have a daddy who would break his knees. But my brothers would do a lot worse if I told them what had happened.

I wouldn't put them in that position.

If Alex Davenport ever laid another finger on me, it would be the last time he touched anyone.

My temper shot through the roof with every stab of pain.

I hate him.

But the thought wasn't just directed at Alex. I hated my father too. For putting me in this position. What man did that to his daughter?

"Miss Hollingsworth."

Father's driver stood dutifully by the car. He opened the back door, which I was expected to get in. And I always did what *he* wanted.

"You ended the evening prematurely."

I'd barely hit the seat before Father started in. "It had run its course."

I was tempted to show him exactly what Alex had done to me. Instead, I gently covered my injured hand with the other. As Hollingsworths, we were expected to handle our own problems. When I'd skinned my knee as a child, it had only taken me once to learn to suck it up.

Never show weakness.

Instead of a Band-Aid and a kiss, I'd received those cold words of wisdom.

"Because you have other plans?"

My stomach dropped. I'd done everything to shake him off my tail to see Cal. Did he know?

"You taught me to walk away when valuable time becomes wasted. He had nothing more to add to this arrangement."

A slight smile, if it could be called such, turned up his thin lips. "Very well. It's best the Davenports don't get too comfortable."

The high I'd felt after seeing Cagan had officially evaporated. I prayed he'd get me out of this disaster, yet felt guilty for even asking in the first place. What if, by marrying me, he missed out on someone special?

Lincoln and Teague had driven home the point that it was never too late in life to find love. *If* that was what a person wanted. Which I didn't.

"They have everything to gain. This deal certainly isn't mutually beneficial." From my standpoint, we had everything to lose. And that was setting aside my personal stake. The Davenports added nothing to the Hollingsworth name.

I didn't care about such things, but my father did. And yet, he was still pushing this deal. This arrangement where his daughter was sold to the highest bidder . . . *Why?*

If there had been a semblance of a smile on his face, it faded. "Do not doubt my decisions."

The burning that radiated from my hand up my arm said I had every reason to.

"I've prepared your room. Until the wedding, you will be at home where you belong."

"My things are at Lincoln's," I protested. Far too quickly, I'd let my thoughts escape.

"And I'll have them collected."

"No, Daddy."

Slowly, he tilted his head. "Is there a reason you choose to stay with your brother over your father?"

A chill skittered up my spine. A million. But I couldn't say that to him.

"I—" An adequate reason to tell him failed to come to mind. I swallowed hard. I couldn't stay with him. He was already stifling. If I was forced to stay with him, I wouldn't be able to breathe without the illusion of freedom. "I'd like another week with him. I'll come stay with you before the wedding."

If my fingers weren't stiff with pain, I'd cross them. Instead, I sent up a prayer, pleading he'd agree to the compromise. Then I'd have to figure out a way to avoid that fresh hell too.

I fashioned my features into one of innocence. "Will you help me pick a dress, Daddy?" I looked down at my hands. The one he'd touched was red and would most certainly be bruised by morning. "Mother isn't here and . . ." I blinked up at him. "It would mean so much to me."

My heart raced. *Please let this distraction work. Please let this distraction work.*

He probably had already selected my dress along with every other detail of the wedding. Mrs. Davenport just *thought* she had a say.

"We'll go shopping after we tour properties tomorrow."

I nearly sagged in relief.

I kissed his cheek. "Thank you, Daddy."

"One week. You'll come home."

This time my smile was somewhat genuine. "Okay." I settled back in my seat, too cocky and too comfortable after my victory. But I had to relish the wins.

We rode in silence until we reached Lincoln's apartment building. A jolt of shock went through me that he'd actually taken me there.

He patted my hand, and I winced.

"I'll collect you, seven a.m."

I nodded and waited for the driver to open the door. When he did, I swung my legs out but twisted back to face my father.

"What would you do if Alex hurt me? Physically."

His expression turned into a cool lethal. "*Has* he hurt you?"

I waved him off. "It was a silly question. See you tomorrow."

As I slid out the back, I nearly stumbled on the curb at what I was almost certain my father said.

"I will hurt him."

CHAPTER TEN

CAL

"I'LL TAKE THE COUCH."

Joe dropped his bag beside it. "No. No. I'll be fine out here."

"You sure?"

"Yeah. I'm sure."

I grabbed a blanket and pillow from the hall closet and handed it to him. "Make yourself at home."

So maybe that wasn't the best choice of words, considering he hated his home at the moment.

"Thanks."

I closed my bedroom door and quickly shed my clothes before I collapsed on the bed. This was the day that kept on giving.

Somehow, I'd talked my brother off the ledge of torching his house, but I swore it was like someone else had taken over his body. An emotionless shell walking around in a daze.

I expected it wouldn't be long until the cops showed up. Hopefully, it would be one of the boys we'd gone to school with, and he'd give Joe a break. They all knew what had happened and that Lee Stanis deserved every punch he got.

An image of Beau beneath me with those brown eyes on fire for me flashed across my brain. I wanted nothing more than to lose myself in her. Forget the shit day I'd had. Forget everything but how she felt wrapped around me.

She'd been a distraction that came along at just the right time. Except *she* was becoming too much of a distraction.

Lately my first instinct, whether things were going right or wrong, was to text her. She didn't expect conversation. Didn't want it. Purely physical. That was how we worked best.

Yet, I wanted some of her snark. Her coldness. And part of me wanted that fight too. Was I a masochist?

I rolled over and punched my pillow. Joe was here. I needed to keep a watch on him, so I couldn't sneak out. And I definitely couldn't bring her here.

Maybe this thing with Joe was a sign. For all my big talk, I'd planned to see her tonight. To bring her here because I couldn't pay for another night in a motel.

Having her in my space was a bad idea. The worst.

Somebody was looking out for me.

I closed my eyes.

Was Joe really going to torch his place? And what was Ma going to do when she found out he'd beaten Lee within an inch of his life?

Bzzz. Bzzz. Bzzz.

I reached for my phone on the nightstand.

"What happened?" My oldest brother's worried voice barreled into my ear.

"He beat the shit out of Lee. I've got him."

"Damn it," Bobby muttered under his breath. "I'll be there in a few."

"No need." I propped against the headboard. "He won't say much anyway."

"You should've brought him here."

"You've got the kids and Michelle. I think it's best if he's away from a happy family environment right now." The last thing Joe needed was a reminder of all the things he *didn't* have.

"Have you called Ma?"

"Are you crazy?" She'd find out soon enough, but I wasn't going to be the one to tell her.

"I'll handle it."

Better him than me. Ma would be furious, especially if Joe went to jail.

"Thanks."

"You call me if anything else happens, okay?" He pulled that older brother card like no one else could.

"Yeah."

I dropped the phone back on the nightstand. Sleep wasn't something I looked forward to, but I needed it. Too bad I was too wired to even think about attempting it.

Bang. Bang. Bang.

I grabbed a shirt off the floor and pulled it over my head. I'd hoped the cops would wait until tomorrow to do this, but that was too much to ask for.

"You could've killed him!"

The screech echoed down the hall. *Shit.* Christina.

Joe blocked the doorway but a flurry of hands and arms flew around him, landing scratches and punches.

"His whole face is broken, Joseph," she screamed. "That's the father of my child."

What a low blow. She had a lot of nerve coming here defending the man she'd cheated with. If she had a decent bone in her body, she'd have taken up for my brother ... her *husband*.

Joe didn't move, just took the blows like he didn't even feel them.

I shoved him out of the way and got between them. She landed a scratch down my cheek. I touched where it stung before I grabbed her wrist.

"You're gonna wake the neighbors," I said evenly.

"Let me go, you asshole." She wiggled and squirmed and kicked with lightning quick moves, especially for a woman who looked ready to pop out a baby any day now.

Son of a ...

"Stop being violent." The woman was making it real hard to keep my cool.

"Tell that to your brother." Her high-pitched voice nearly burst my eardrums. "You Calhouns are thick as thieves. None of you care about your wives. Just the station."

There were truths and lies in what she said. We were tight, and at one point in time, she'd loved being part of that. She had a welcoming and loving mother-in-law, five brothers-in-law who would have dropped anything for her. Because that was what family did. But we cared about our family as much as we did the firehouse. And Joe? He was one of the best of both families.

"If you were unhappy, you should've talked to Joe instead of screwing his best friend," I said calmly.

"I *did* try to talk to him!" She thrashed and kicked again, but this time I dodged her.

Doors opened on both sides of the hall.

"Will you shut up?" Old Man Casey threw up his hands. "Some of us are trying to sleep."

Mrs. Peters just peered from next door like she was watching a soap opera. She hadn't even bothered to remove her rollers or nightcap.

"You shut up," Christina yelled back.

Old Man Casey pointed at me. "If you don't get this broad under control, I'm calling the cops."

"Already did!" somebody yelled from downstairs.

Great.

"Haven't you done enough?" I let her go and slammed the door in her face.

Bang. Bang. Bang.

"Cal! You open this door right now. Caaaalllll!"

Joe hadn't moved, still standing beside me. He was silent. Unmoving as a statue.

Wham. Wham. Wham.

"Joe Calhoun, I haaateee you!"

Is this what he's been living with all this time?

Christina was always a loud mouth, but I put up with her because my brother loved her.

His head hung and he was withdrawn. This man had saved more

than one of his brothers at the station from fires. He was a leader. In command.

And that woman had reduced him to this shell.

It was so wrong.

Blue lights flashed. I pulled back the curtain. A squad car had just rolled up in front of the building. I squinted to make out who was here.

Egan and McCreedie. Thank goodness for small mercies. Joe and I saw them both a lot on the job.

Bam. Bam. Bam.

"Cal, I swear if you don't open this door!"

"Christina, you gotta hold it down." McCreedie's muffled voice came through the door.

"Oh great. You'll both side with him. I want some objective cops."

I put a hand to my forehead and squeezed. Maybe it was better if Joe was zoned out and didn't hear any of this.

"We're not siding with anyone, but right now you're the one disturbing the peace," Egan said.

"Get her out of here," Old Man Casey shouted.

"I'm not going anywhere until Joseph Calhoun explains why he almost killed Lee."

Really? That was pretty much self-explanatory.

"Christina, if you come with us now and promise not to cause another scene, we'll let you go."

"We'll drive you home. This stress isn't good for the baby. A night in a cell wouldn't be either."

She mumbled something I couldn't hear. There was blessed silence for several seconds and then what sounded like heavy footsteps on the stairs.

Tap. Tap. Tap.

The knocking was faint. *Am I supposed to answer that?*

I cracked open the door.

Egan rolled his eyes. "I don't think she's coming back." He glanced behind me toward Joe. "And we know exactly why you did what you did."

"Thanks for coming by." I kept my body wedged between the door and the frame.

"Try to keep it down," he said with a smirk before giving me a fist-bump. "All right, people. Show's over." He jogged down the stairs.

Doors closed one by one until I was the only person looking into the hall. I rubbed the back of my neck. Weren't we too old for this mess?

"Sorry for the trouble," Joe said quietly.

Was he for real? His wife had turned into an entitled, selfish bitch and he was apologizing?

I closed the door and shook his shoulders. "You didn't do anything wrong."

He refused to look at me.

I turned him in the direction of the short hall. "Take my room. You'll sleep better."

Like a robot he did as I said, trudging toward my bedroom. I grabbed my phone, keys, wallet, and some clothes.

"I have to be at the station early," Joe said.

I dropped his bag on the floor. "Sleep well."

I waited until he sat on the bed before I closed the door. What a night. I sank onto the sofa and leaned my head against the back. I'd never sleep now. I was too amped up.

Had all of this really happened? I couldn't believe Christina had cheated on Joe in the first place. She should've had the decency to be honest. Finding out she didn't love him anymore would've been hard on him, but this? It was a disaster. Beyond cruel.

And maybe I didn't live in that house with them, but Joe had been a good husband. He didn't deserve the humiliation. He'd have to live with the evidence of her indiscretions for the rest of his life.

For such a big city, it was a small community. He'd see that kid or Christina and Lee, and it would be a sucker punch every time.

For once, I couldn't fix the mess.

I hated that.

My phone burned in my palm. I wanted to give Old Man Casey another reason to call the cops with a noise complaint. Beau's cries of pleasure as I forgot everything else but what it felt like to be inside her.

You can't leave Joe.

I opened the text app.

You don't have the money for a hotel.

I pressed the screen to our last conversation.

Need you now.

I practically felt the words. She'd showed me just how much she'd needed me. Beau was bold. Unafraid to go after what she wanted. And since we'd started this tryst, I'd demanded of her what I wanted too.

My thumbs hovered over the screen. *I can't bring her here.*

The phone vibrated in my hand.

Change of scene.

A second later an address on West 56th appeared.

I put on my jeans and a fresh shirt before I shoved my wallet in my back pocket. For a minute I stood in front of the coffee table, looking between the front door and my bedroom door. I hesitated.

What are you gonna do? Cuddle Joe all night?

If I were in his position, I'd want me to go.

You're thinking with the wrong head, Cal.

I swiped my keys off the coffee table and slipped out the front door.

CHAPTER ELEVEN

BEAU

NO ANSWER.

You aren't supposed to be the one initiating contact.

I couldn't help myself. I needed his touch to replace Alex's filthy one.

I kicked off my shoes and propped my feet on the coffee table.

Being a beck-and-call girl wasn't exactly me. I knew what I was doing. So what if the side effect was a little—okay, a lot—of pleasure? It had been a long time and using him to blow off some much-needed steam was as good a form of stress relief as I could think of.

If I could convince Cagan to marry me, I'd be headed back to London soon. This would all be nothing but a memory. And hopefully Cal would feel half of what he'd made me feel all those years ago.

I can't sleep with Cagan.

Not because he wasn't attractive. And it probably would be quite good. But I . . . I couldn't cross that line. What was I planning to do? Ask him to become celibate to save my ass?

I can't.

We could work out an arrangement. It wasn't as if I planned on sharing a bed with him. Maybe a house, but . . .

In my desperation, I hadn't thought this through at all. I could live with it for a few years, but I had so much more to gain. What I couldn't live with was putting my friend through the restraint of a marriage he didn't want.

I grabbed my phone.

Three dots had been flashing for almost an hour, but no response.

I searched for Cagan's contact and dialed.

"By all means, call me at any hour."

He sounded wide awake. With the time difference it was almost six a.m. in London and I was sure he hadn't adjusted to New York time so quickly.

"I appreciate that," I said saucily. "About what I proposed earlier—"

"Nice choice of words."

Jackass.

"Forget it."

"Have you already found someone else? You wound me."

I could just picture his hand over his heart in mock despair.

"You'll get over it." A smile cracked my face.

"Eventually. Maybe." He was quiet a second. "I understand your predicament far better than I wish to. If you need to have a chat, I'm here."

"Thanks." I was grateful for my friend. "Same goes."

"If any solutions come to mind, I'll ring you."

Knock. Knock. Knock.

I dropped my feet to the floor.

"You'd better think fast."

I hung up, tossed my phone aside, and rushed to the door. Hand on the doorknob, I hesitated.

Don't look so eager, Beau.

But I was. And I ignored the warning signals going off in my head about that.

I barely had the door open when Cal pushed inside. He kicked it shut and grabbed me by the waist, pulling me flush against him.

Something turbulent and dangerous and greedy flashed in his dark eyes. *Don't kiss me. You can't kiss me. You know the rules.*

That turbulence appeared ready to tell my rules to kiss its ass.

Why is he staring?

Normally we went straight to ripping off clothes. This . . . it was too intense.

He grabbed my injured hand, and I hissed at the bolt of pain.

His expression turned lethal. He lifted my hand, putting it under the overhead light. Deep purple had already formed on my skin.

"What happened?"

The demand was rough. I blinked at him. We didn't exchange pleasantries. No *how was your day, dear* or anything personal. All of our conversation revolved around commands of pleasure.

"It's nothing," I brushed off, diving for the hem of his shirt. I needed to get this back on track. Back to purely physical.

He circled my uninjured wrist, bringing my movements to a halt.

"Doesn't look like nothing."

That stare. It made me forget completely about my bruises because I felt too much chaos racing through my body.

I shrugged. "I slammed it—"

"*Don't* lie to me."

Oh no. I poked a finger into his solid chest. "You lost any say over what I do a long time ago. Now do you want to make me scream or leave? Your choice."

He stalked over to the nightstand and picked up the phone. "I need a bucket of ice."

Cal was back in front of me, his tender touch of my hand a direct contrast to the ferocity on his face. He led me to the sofa and sat so that I had no choice but to sit beside him.

"Can you move it?" With the slightest motion, he brushed his thumb over my swollen pinky.

"When did you become a doctor?"

I scooted away. This wasn't part of our arrangement. He didn't get to act like he cared when I knew otherwise.

His jaw set as his eyes demanded an answer.

I sighed in frustration, mostly with myself. "I'd rather not."

"Did you feel anything crack?"

Only every bone in my hand. But I wasn't going to say that.

"Did I dial the wrong number? Because I'm pretty sure I didn't text you for an examination." I angled to put some distance between us.

Gently, he pressed on all my fingers as if testing them, for what I didn't know. When he touched my pinky, I sank my teeth into my lower lip and grunted.

A light knock on the door had him on his feet at a speed a man of his size shouldn't be capable of. When he was across the room and out of my space, I took my first full breath since he'd arrived.

He grabbed the ice and shoved the door closed, tossing the bucket on the coffee table, so that he only held the bag of ice. He moved with a confidence most men didn't have. But he'd always been that way, even thirteen years ago when we'd first met.

Now it was different.

More potent.

Maybe age had made him that way. Or life.

He wasn't like so many of the other men I encountered. I couldn't run over Garrett Calhoun.

He turned up his palm and situated my hand on top of it on his thigh.

I balled my fist when he settled the bag of ice on my wounded hand. *Cold. Cold. Cold.*

I shoved down how miserable I was and put on a brave face.

"Your dad do that to you?"

I gaped at the question. "No. Why would you think that?"

"I've seen hands slammed in doors. That ain't it." He flicked his chin toward me. "You used to talk about what an ass he was to you and your brothers. Seemed like a logical choice."

He remembered? I barely did. When we'd been together, I hadn't wanted to taint our time with all the stress my father put on me. Back then, he'd been pressuring me about the company. About what he wanted me to do.

I guess I'd unloaded that on Cal more than I thought. Maybe because at one point, more than a decade ago, I'd thought I meant more to him. I'd thought we were more.

"He's never physically hurt me."

I clamped my mouth closed. That wasn't his business. He didn't get to know personal things about me anymore. My body. That was all he had access to.

Which apparently included my injured hand.

"I wanna know who did."

A streak of fear skittered down my spine. Cal . . . he wasn't afraid to get his hands dirty. He would snap Alex Davenport in half with one hand.

And while I certainly had no interest in protecting Alex, I saw no point in divulging unnecessary information to Cal. This was a one-off. He seemed to care, but he had a long time ago too.

I'd fallen for it then. I wasn't going to now.

"This has been on long enough."

He stopped me before I could remove the ice bag. "Don't think so."

I closed my eyes and willed patience to come to me. I was so tired of men telling me what to do. My father. My brothers. Alex. Garrett —no, *Cal*.

"Just go." My words had no fire. They were flat and tired. Just like me.

"Can't do that."

"Sure you can. It's easy. You get up, open the door, and walk out." I glared at him. "You're very good at that."

You just couldn't keep your mouth shut, could you? I wanted him to think I'd forgotten about what he'd done to me. Instead, I'd just proved I'd never let it go.

His nostrils flared, but he made no move. Instead, we sat in stony silence, glaring at one another.

His face had more lines than it had all those years ago. The hardened edge he'd had seemed more defined now. Like the innocence of youth had worn off and life ripped off the veil of *anything was possible* and replaced it with a real-world view that *sometimes it was ugly*.

His hair was still jet-black. He'd been solid muscle in his twenties and still was. But he'd filled out. I knew from experience his hands were more calloused, and he could use them in expert ways. When we'd been together before, he'd never been shy. Now, he was just more man.

Time had been his friend.

As badly as I hated to admit it, he was more devastating today than he had been the first time I'd laid eyes on him.

When I'd fired off that text with the address for the hotel, I hadn't had a staring contest in mind. Nor a walk down memory lane of just how much better he looked and how much more he affected me now.

"I'M GLAD YOU CAME."

Teague grabbed two beers from the cooler and offered me one.

"I can't believe you're almost out of the fire academy." I took a long sip, surveying the crowd of his new friends.

A couple of them argued over the grill, a few others played cards, and yet another group laughed like one of them had told the funniest joke ever.

"Let me introduce you to everybody." He slung an arm around my shoulders and steered me toward the laughing group.

"Yo, Hollingsworth!" one of them shouted as he lifted a drink.

"Yo. Burke." Teague lifted his beer in response.

"Who's the babe?"

"My baby sister, so you better be on your best behavior."

I cringed. It was a toss-up who was more overprotective. Teague or Lincoln.

I elbowed him in the side and waved.

"Come sit by me." Burke patted the bench next to him and grinned.

Teague tightened his hold on me. "Not a chance in hell."

"Aw, come on. I'm a nice guy." He winked. "Sometimes."

"I wouldn't let my brother sit next to him."

The deep voice floated over us from behind, and I felt it in my stomach.

Teague and I turned. Tall, dark, and handsome wasn't even close to this guy. Tall was accurate. Dangerous. And beautiful in a rugged kind of way.

Teague was a chameleon. He fit in with any group, even if he was more refined than this one.

This one? He had a roughness about him that could never be filed to a smooth edge. A coolness that set him apart. Yet a warmth that made me want to see just how hot he burned.

Teague laughed. "Me neither."

But I stared. I'd been taught to school my visible reactions by the best, but no one could've prepared me for him.

"Hollingsworth, Murano here thinks steak goes on after burgers. Tell him he's wrong," one of the guys by the grill called.

Teague lifted a brow. "I'd better go see about those two before we end up with nothing to eat." He slapped Rugged in the arm. "Watch out for my sister a minute."

Rugged lifted his chin.

"I don't need a nanny," I said as Teague stepped out of earshot.

"Good thing, 'cause I ain't entertaining no little girls."

I swallowed hard, unable to take my eyes off him. His throat worked as he downed a swig of beer.

He smirked when he caught me staring. "Baby sister got a name?"

"Beau." It came out breathless and a little bit needy with none of the power I usually used behind the word.

Great. I was a fawning teenage girl instead of college-educated woman. A little girl. Just like he'd insinuated. And he knew exactly the effect he had on me. It was in that smug expression.

"Garrett Calhoun." His dark eyes blazed into mine. "Everybody calls me Cal."

"I'm *not* everybody."

"You certainly ain't."

I SNATCHED my hand away and bolted from the sofa, singed by thoughts of the first time we'd met. He was still rugged, aloof, and dangerous. And I was still a little girl wowed by his spectacular presence.

You're a fool, Beau.

It didn't matter how many years of experience I'd gained. I hadn't mastered my emotions or anything when it came to Garrett Calhoun.

And he'd just proved how not in control I was.

CHAPTER TWELVE

CAL

"IF YOU WANNA BE stubborn and hurt tomorrow, that's on you."

I stood, towering over her since she was in bare feet.

"It already hurts." She snapped her mouth closed as if she hadn't wanted to admit that.

I snatched the ice bag off the couch and put it back on her hand. "We should have it X-rayed."

We. Not we. *She*. She should have it X-rayed.

I should get the hell out of here before I start blathering about how beautiful she is or about this mess with Joe or all of the things we had no business discussing.

Action. That was what we were about. And I couldn't take any when she was injured.

My rage ramped to a boil. She hadn't slammed her hand into anything. And when I found out who did this, whether it was her daddy or the president of the United States, they wouldn't ever touch Beau or any other woman again.

Stay out of it, Cal.

I was already in it.

"I'm. Fine."

"That nasty looking bruise says otherwise."

"Why did I text you?" She threw up the arm I wasn't currently holding in place.

"Because you wanted me to make you scream."

"In pleasure," she said through her teeth. "Not anger."

"I'm an ass, but if you think I'm going to risk injuring you further just so you can have an orgasm, you got another thing coming."

"Don't act like you care."

She might as well have slapped me. I should go. Get out of here. Delete her number and block it for good measure.

Because it had only taken a few weeks of her back in my life to prove just how much I'd been lying to myself that I *didn't* care.

I'd never stopped.

And that wasn't good for either of us. Especially me.

I never should've gotten tangled up in her sheets.

"Get on the bed."

She lifted her chin. "I'm not so sure I'm in the mood anymore."

"I won't ask again."

She hesitated only a second before leaving the ice bag dangling in my grasp and crawling onto the mattress.

I flipped off lights until the only thing left glowing was the lamp on the nightstand. She was so pretty sitting in the center of the bed. No, pretty wasn't right. She— *Don't think about it.*

I focused on her hand. Even from here, I could see the purple had darkened.

I kicked off my shoes and settled in beside her. I clasped her hand, set the ice on top, and switched off the lamp.

"What are you doing, Cal?"

I hated she called me Cal. She'd never done it before, but I got the message loud and clear. I was just like everybody else to her now.

"If you won't look after yourself, I will." I nestled into the pillows. They were better than mine. I'd probably have to take out a loan to pay for this hotel room. Because I sure as hell wasn't letting her do it.

She shifted, though it was too dark to see her face. "Oh no, no, no. This has an expiration date. It's straight-up sex. And we aren't taking it any further."

"Making sure you keep ice on your hand isn't a marriage proposal."

She made a slight choking noise. I switched on the light. Her cheeks were red, and I was tempted to get out of bed because she looked ready to murder me.

"Just go, Cal," she said again. There she went, calling me Cal again.

"The sooner you go to sleep, the sooner I'll be out of here." Gently, I pushed her shoulder, making sure to keep the ice balanced on her hand.

She flopped back and stared at the ceiling. "Fabulous. I'll die of frostbite next to a man I hate."

"That's better than dying alone."

The silence was almost too much to take. Neither the air conditioning nor a neighbor made a sound. There was always street noise or someone listening to music or arguing in my building. This place was quieter than a tomb.

And why had death suddenly become the theme?

"I can't sleep on my back," she huffed.

I knew that.

But it was buried so deep in the recesses of my mind, I'd forgotten.

I got out of bed. "Scoot this way."

The covers rustled as she did what I said. There were small miracles.

I bumped my knee on the corner of the mattress as I rounded it, but managed to make it to her empty spot.

It was a mistake.

The pillow already smelled like her. Something I'd never been able to figure out exactly what it was. There was a hint of sweet mixed with . . . spicy. Not that overbearing floral perfume crap that was strong enough to make a man gag.

"Put your hand on my stomach."

This time, there was a beat of hesitation, but her heat shifted toward me, and her hand singed my stomach through my shirt.

I settled the ice pack on top of her hand and sucked in when the cold pierced my skin.

I'd never admit it, but she was right. She may damn well get frostbite from this.

My arm was pinned between us. It was uncomfortable as could be. Carefully, I moved, slipping it underneath her neck. I cradled her next to me, a mistake I hadn't made in all the times I'd been with her in the past few weeks.

I felt more exposed now than I had naked. And we'd spent most of our time with no clothes on.

"WHERE ARE WE GOING?"

There was a hint of excitement in her voice as we crept up the side stairwell of my pop's fire station. It was mine too now. I couldn't get used to the fact I'd finally made it through the academy.

I put a finger to my lips and squeezed her hand. It was slender and delicate and warm in mine.

If we got caught, Pop would cover for me, but if Teague found out, he'd bury me for sneaking around with his baby sister.

Some risks were worth taking.

When we reached the top of the stairs, I quietly turned the handle on the door with my free hand, barely keeping the blanket tucked under my arm in place.

The summer air was thick and hot when it hit us. If Beau minded, she didn't say anything.

"You afraid of heights?" I looked up the metal ladder affixed to the exterior brick.

She gave me a look like I was ridiculous and climbed the tiny rungs in high heels like it was her job. When she stepped over the top, I followed.

She spun, taking in the view of the Bronx. We weren't skyscraper high. The station wasn't even the tallest building around. But it was like being above the city while still right in the middle of it.

I spread out the blanket and tugged her down with me. She was too fancy to be lying on an old blanket on the rooftop, yet she did it with grace and elegance. Just like she did everything else.

I lay back and opened my arm. She snuggled against me, and I forgot about how hot it was or that my shift started at seven in the morning or my rent was three days late.

I couldn't focus on anything but her.

"My pop brought me up here when I was a kid." I'd thought it was the most special place in the world. With five other brothers, it was hard to get time to myself with him. But he'd made it for all of us. And this was our spot.

I'd never shared it with anybody. Never thought to.

"The stars seem closer here."

Compared to where, I didn't know. But they were putting on a show, unobstructed by clouds and smog.

I ran my fingers up and down her side. She shivered and burrowed closer against me. Like she needed me.

For that moment, I let myself believe she did. I had nothing to offer her she didn't already have. Nothing that she couldn't get.

You shoulda left her alone, Cal.

Like I had a choice.

I wouldn't think about that now. She was here. And I was a king with her in my arms.

"Can you sleep on your back?"

"You thinking of spending the night here?"

She propped her chin on my chest. "Maybe."

"I can sleep any way."

She tilted her head. "I can't. Not even when I'm dead tired."

"Sounds like a challenge to me." I rolled on top of her, hovering my face inches above hers. "Maybe you need me to wear you out."

Her eyes slightly widened, but there was so much want in them it nearly knocked me back. I'd taken her on dates, ones I could afford, and it was becoming an almost nightly addiction. Mostly we drove around the city, talking and listening to music with the windows rolled down.

This had been going on for three months.

I'd held her hand. Talked to her on the phone like we were in high school. But I hadn't touched her.

Somebody owed me a medal for that.

"Maybe I do," she rasped.

I propped on my forearms on either side of her head. There wasn't a more *beautiful thing on the planet. I hadn't seen much of it outside of the city, but I was sure of that.*

I inched closer.

Her lips parted.

I nuzzled her nose, breathing in that scent that was uniquely Beau. She was a queen, meant to be chauffeured and dripping in jewels. Not sneaking around with some chump who just wanted to be a fireman.

But I had her now.

And I couldn't let go.

Her mouth was soft and sweet when I captured it. She wrapped her arms around me in a hold that felt like a claim. She darted her hands under my shirt and scraped her nails down my back.

I hissed and lost all sense of control. My kiss turned hard, like a brand I wouldn't let her forget. And she welcomed it, kissing me back with as much as I gave. Her tongue swept into mine, and I groaned as I pressed my body against hers. I wanted her. I'd wanted her since I first met her, but I'd known then she was way out of my league. Yet, being with her, no matter what we did together, never felt like that.

"Garrett," *she whispered as her fingers wove into my hair.*

Nobody called me that. Not even Ma. And when Beau did . . . I kissed her like I'd never have another chance. Like she was the only one I ever wanted. Like she was the best gift I'd ever received.

"Say it again."

It wasn't smart to let her know exactly what my name on her lips did to me, but I didn't care about anything but hearing it again.

"Garrett."

You own me, baby sister. There's not one thing I won't do for you.

I STARED AT THE CEILING. Beau's breathing evened. She held me tighter in her sleep. At first, I'd called her baby sister as a reminder to myself she was off-limits. She was Teague's sister. No matter how I tried to keep her firmly in that camp, it hadn't helped. Then the nickname had stuck.

Baby sister got a name?

I'd called her that from the very first time we'd met, and it had been an endearment the whole time, even when I thought it hadn't.

And as I lay there with a numb stomach, I realized it didn't matter how much time passed.

Some things never changed.

CHAPTER THIRTEEN

BEAU

YOU CROSSED A LINE.

A giant red one that shocked with high voltage and permanently singed.

When I'd started sleeping with Cal, I hadn't meant literal sleeping. And damn him if that wasn't the best rest I'd had in I couldn't remember how long. Even with a gimp hand.

Which was stiff and sore, but would've been a lot worse if it weren't for his tyrant-like insistence.

He couldn't do things like that. Couldn't make me feel cared for and protected.

If I needed that, I could count on my brothers or my friends.

But it was different with Cal.

"Morning, Beau."

I blinked up at Eric, who'd snuck into the kitchen without me hearing. Or maybe I was just in a daze. Millie followed close on his heels. That dog was protective of my best friend's brother.

"Hey, Eric. Can you forgive me for missing our piano lesson?" Guilt swirled through me. How was I going to teach him with my hand in the shape it was?

"Sure. Things happen," he said easily.

I side-hugged him. "Thanks, pal. Let me know when you can fit me in that busy schedule of yours."

Hopefully it interfered with wedding planning and whatever else my father had planned for my future.

"Want to make deliveries with us today?"

I'd helped out when Lexie hadn't been able to drive for a few days. It had been fun to help deliver their gourmet dog food. A nice change.

"Actually, I gotta jet. My father is picking me up"—I checked my watch—"any minute now."

"He needs a hug."

My brows shot to my hairline. No one would've ever thought that. Except Eric, who had the biggest genuine heart.

Maybe it would loosen up Father. I just wasn't sure I was brave enough to try it. Snakes weren't meant to be hugged.

"Could be." I tugged on his bow tie. "Give everyone kisses for me. Maybe I'll see you tonight?"

"We'll text you."

I laughed and grabbed my keys. There was nothing like a dose of Eric to brighten a day. Even one I dreaded.

How's your hand?

IT WAS BARELY AFTER EIGHT. He had no business texting me in daylight hours. Especially not with his . . . *concern*.

"There's a his and hers walk-in closet—"

"I've seen enough," I said, clearing the message and dimming my phone.

Father lifted a brow. I shook my head. At eight thousand square feet, this apartment wasn't big enough for Alex and me to cohabitate.

Not that we were going to.

If we were actually purchasing a property, I wanted it to be one with a high rate of return, not just something I'd settled on because it had to be done quickly.

I'd bought property in less time than this. But it was senseless to rush into a decision.

"Thank you for allowing us to view the apartment. It truly is lovely," I said, pasting a smile on my face.

Hers faltered, uncertain if I liked it or hated it. "Of course," she said brightly as she cut her eyes to my father. Always looking to him for the final say.

I tucked my arm in his elbow. "Ready, Daddy."

If she wanted to play games, I'd show her who had the ultimate say. And if calling him Daddy to give the illusion that I was still his little girl did that, so be it.

"Of course, my dear."

As soon as we were out of her sight, I released my light hold on him. This was the third property we'd seen so far. I hated all of them. They were stuffy and pretentious and didn't feel like a home.

You don't plan to live in any of them.

None of them gave me that little flurry of excitement in my stomach. The one that always told me *I'm the one, pick me.*

It had only led me astray once. After that, I'd become more careful. If I'd lost all trust in my gut, I would've missed out on a lot of tremendous opportunities.

"There are only so many properties on the market," Father said as he held open the car door for me.

"And this one isn't it." I didn't give the apartment building another glance. "Do we have anything else to see?"

"Let's select your dress while I make arrangements."

"Brilliant." Wedding dress shopping wasn't something I should be doing with him. Lexie, Eric, Pepper, and Miss Adeline should be coming with me. And it shouldn't be something I dreaded.

But this was Father's charade. I was his puppet. And I'd pretend I was going to wear whatever he wished, though today was the last time I ever intended to put it on.

"Is there a particular reason you refused to come home where you belong yet spent the night in a hotel on West 56th?"

I stiffened but prayed he didn't see it. In my haste and pain, I'd been careless and taken a taxi straight there from Lincoln's. Had he seen Cal?

For once I was grateful he'd arrived so much later than I did.

"I'd heard good things about it. It has potential. We should consider making the owner an offer."

"And a good time to preview the property is at midnight?"

He wasn't even trying to hide that he'd followed me. Or had me followed. Whatever it was he did.

"When someone is aware you're coming, they hide things. That gave me an opportunity to see the real state of affairs. My schedule only allows for so many engagements, so I went when I had a free moment." I refreshed my lipstick. "I very much like it."

His jaw ticked. "The hotel is not for sale."

I dropped the tube back into my purse. "*Everything* is for sale."

CHAPTER FOURTEEN

CAL

SIX HOURS. No answer.

I looked at my phone for what had to be the hundredth time before I jogged up the steps to Ma's.

It was my day off. She'd mentioned in passing the back door lock was sticking, so I'd come to fix it, even though she hadn't asked.

She'd feed me in the process.

Thank God, after what that room set me back last night. Looked like Ma would be seeing a bit more of me in the near-distant future.

Bzzz. Bzzz. Bzzz.

Was she finally calling me back?

Aaron.

I deflated as I answered the phone. "What's up?"

"You got a second?"

"I'm headed into Ma's." I hesitated with my hand on the doorknob.

"I need five hundred."

I leaned against the wall. *Not again.* "Roy told me Quinn came by the bar. I thought after the last five you were done."

"It was a sure-fire bet, man. I just—"

"Lost. Again." Irritation coursed through me. My brother had developed a gambling problem, and I was enabling it by continually bailing him out.

But I'd done it all our lives. He'd never been good with money and I wasn't going to let him suffer.

"Yeah." He sounded dejected.

"Come by Ma's. I'll spot you, but this has got to stop. You hear me?"

"Thanks, Cal. You're the best." He'd gone from down to exuberant in seconds. "And I hear you."

He hung up. I stood there for a second, knowing this wouldn't be the last time. How the hell was I going to help him? And I needed to put in for some overtime.

I had a thousand dollars stashed in my old room upstairs. It was my savings account that continually was depleted. But if it helped my family, that was all that mattered. What else did I have to work for anyway?

I pushed off the wall and rang the bell to let her know I was there, but let myself in. "Ma."

"In the kitchen, Cal."

The furniture in the living room was the same as it had been since Pop had surprised her with a new set when I was in high school. It was worn but still in good shape for its age. She never said anything about wanting something new, and I wasn't sure she did.

Ma held on to every piece of my father she could get her hands on.

We all did.

She stood at the stove, stirring something in a pan. Did she sleep there?

I hugged her from behind and kissed her cheek. "Smells good. Always does."

"Did they find out what happened to Joe's house?"

I dropped my arms and stumbled back. "What are you talking about?"

She turned, still stirring without looking. "His house burned down this morning."

"And nobody thought to mention it to me?"

He'd been gone when I got back home just before dawn, but he'd said he had an early morning. I wasn't on today, but with the way news spread, I couldn't believe no one had called. Especially not my family.

"I'm sorry. I thought Aaron told you." She banged the wooden spoon on the side of the pot and set it down. "First that woman I called a daughter cheated on him and now this," she shouted. Then looked at me, pleading. "Hasn't my boy been through enough?"

Did she know about the fight? Beat down was more like it. I wasn't going to bring it up unless she did.

I'd seen people lose everything to fire more times than I liked to think about. Maybe things weren't great at Joe's house, but if it was all gone... that would do something to a person.

Memories, a lifetime of things he'd collected, precious possessions that had been Pop's, photos... none of it could be replaced. At least he was okay, wasn't he?

"Have you talked to Joe?"

"He said he's fine. Another call came in and he had to go." She pulled two plates from the cabinet above her head.

I shooed her out of the way. "Let me get that."

I took them from her hands and set them on the counter. It was a relief to hear she'd spoken to him and he wasn't hurt.

"Ramona said she heard it was arson." She scooped chicken cutlets and gravy onto the plates. "Christina has lost her mind."

I stilled as I grabbed one. "*She* set the house on fire?"

What the hell was wrong with that woman? She'd destroyed my brother and now destroyed the house. I didn't want to know what was next.

"Well, it's not official, but after the scene she caused at your place..." She gave me that stern mother look that still made me nervous. "You should've called me."

A pit formed in my stomach. I didn't like keeping stuff from her, but she didn't need the stress, especially when there was nothing she could do about it.

"I didn't want to worry you, Ma. The neighbors called the cops and she left. It was over almost before it started." But not quick enough to keep her from doing even more damage to Joe first.

He'd been so dejected. So robotic. Like all that was left was his body and he was operating on autopilot. I couldn't stand he was hurting so. I wanted to take it from him and carry it so he didn't have to.

"You go pick up Joe after his shift and bring him to me. He needs to be home. I don't care how old he is."

I wasn't sure that was a good idea. Our mother was a great lady. The best. And she loved us in spite of what heathens we were. But she'd hover.

"He stayed with me last night."

She patted my hand. "And you're a good boy for looking out for him. But that's no place for two people to live." She hopped up. "Oh, I forgot the bread."

In seconds, she had the fresh garlic loaf on the table. She sliced a piece and put it on my plate. "You should come home too. Help me keep an eye out on Joe. Then I can make sure you're fed properly. You look thin."

I glanced down, not sure what she was talking about. My diet lately hadn't been the greatest, but I was still in good shape.

"This is good, Ma." Too heavy for lunch, but beggars couldn't be choosers. And it was the best thing I'd had to eat since I was here last.

"Since you won't find a nice girl, your mother will just have to keep feeding you."

Somehow, I didn't think that was a hardship on her.

She forked some salad, then set it down. "I need you to watch out for Joe." She pushed her mostly uneaten plate of food away. "I don't have a good feeling. If she could cheat on my Joe, go ballistic like it was his fault, and then burn their house down, I don't know what else she's capable of."

I swallowed a bite of bread. "What are you getting at?"

"I think she might kill him."

CHAPTER FIFTEEN

BEAU

"WE HAVE dinner with the Davenports tomorrow at seven."

It was the parting shot on this hellacious day. I'd been measured and poked and prodded. Normally, I would've enjoyed shopping for beautiful clothes, but this had been torture.

Father had selected a dress that was stunning, but I hated.

The home search had extended into tomorrow.

And I had a pile of messages to return from the office in London. I'd never been away for this extended period of time. I had a team that was more than capable, but without me there, there were little fires everywhere. A new property in an area we'd had our eyes on had come up for sale and we needed to move now. A clerical error at the bank caused funds to be delayed on a closing. And a couple I'd allowed to continue working for us despite it going against company policy had fought in the lobby and cost us a relationship with a potential new development partner.

Like Lincoln, my favorite aspect of our business was the property hunt. But being at the helm of our European division meant somehow everything landed on my desk. I was referee, CEO, advisor, therapist, problem-solver . . . and I wouldn't change any of it.

"You and I had plans for the art gallery opening." I pretended to protest. Neither event sounded like a good time.

"And we'll attend afterward. It will be good for you to be seen with Alex. To get people warm to the idea of you as a couple."

He meant for *me* to get used to it.

I might not even have to fake an illness to get out of it because I suddenly wasn't feeling well.

"Thank you for the dress. It's lovely."

I'd kept up the charade of adoring daughter the entire day, and I was exhausted from it.

"You'll be beautiful when I walk you down the aisle."

My hand froze on my purse strap. *Noooo.* No, I didn't want that at all. I hadn't thought that far ahead, but everything rebelled in me at that idea. Not just because I didn't want to marry Alex. *If* I ever did find someone I wanted to take that leap with, it wasn't my father I pictured at my side.

Lincoln and Teague were.

The car door opened. I gave my father a tight smile as I got out.

"Beau?" Had he not already had the last word? "I trust you won't be looking at transient properties again in the middle of the night."

I didn't reply.

He didn't want one anyway. He'd made his point.

THE APARTMENT WAS quiet when I stepped inside.

I loved my family and wasn't much for silence, but I was grateful for the moment alone, no matter how short-lived it might be.

I ran a bath while I undressed. Steam filled the bathroom, and I drew in a deep, calming breath.

You will figure this out.

And I would. I just needed a minute of peace.

My phone buzzed. I was tempted to ignore it but couldn't resist reading the notification on the screen.

Be home late. We stopped by the dog shelter. Lincoln went insane. Don't ask. At the kitchen now to make a double batch of food for tomorrow.

I didn't want to know what Lexie meant by "Lincoln went insane."

Do I need to come by?

Please say no. Please say no. It was wrong to think that. If my friend needed me, I'd be there.

We're good. And he's fine. He just wrote a giant check and threatened them not to ever kill a dog.

I wasn't surprised. My seemingly unfeeling brother had a big heart. I'd kept that secret a long time, but Lexie and Eric had unearthed it. If Lincoln had a say, and he did, every animal shelter in this city would have whatever they needed to operate without hurting another living creature.

I sent a thumbs-up emoji and sank into the tub. The water was hot, too hot, but I slid in up to my chin. I closed my eyes, willing the entire wasted day to evaporate.

My phone buzzed again, this time with a call. Lexie must have more to report on what Lincoln had done.

"You haven't answered my text."

The ferocious growl thundered in my ear before I had a chance to speak. My eyelids flew open.

Cal.

He hadn't called me . . . I wouldn't think about the last time he had.

"I have a hand that feels like it's been through a meat grinder. That's not exactly conducive to texting."

He grunted like he was some sort of primitive caveman. Strangely, it got his point across loud and clear. My answer was unsatisfactory to him.

"Put more ice on it."

"By all means, tell me what to do, doctor." I rolled my eyes and leaned my head back again.

"I mean it."

"I'm sure you do." If he were here, I'd give him my favorite fake smile. And he'd return his best grimace.

"How's the bruising?"

"Will you stop?"

He was turning this into something it wasn't. Kissing wasn't allowed and phone calls were quickly moving their way up the list.

"Excuse the hell out of me for wanting to make sure you're okay. My mistake."

I sat up. Water splashed over the side of the tub.

"Don't you dare, Garrett Calhoun. You gave up your say over anything to do with me, quite willingly as I recall."

"And you've given your body right back to me, quite willingly as I recall."

Bastard.

He was right.

"Is this some sort of sick mind game?" He'd toyed with me all those years ago. I'd been too infatuated to see it. Too . . . *don't you even think it, Beau.*

"You're the one playing games, baby sister."

That nickname. He'd called me that from the first time we met. Something inside me always reacted. This time it was longing with a heavy dose of pain and anger.

"*I* just wanted sex. *You're* the one dragging other garbage into this."

"Since when is hating to see you hurt a crime?"

"Since you took the position as king of doing it." I hung up. He'd riled me up to the point of admitting a truth I didn't even speak to myself any longer.

I'd just handed over more power to the man who still held all the shattered pieces of my heart.

Bzzz. Bzzz. Bzzz.

I stabbed the ignore button on my phone. Spending any amount of time in New York had been a bad idea. One I'd been forced into.

Because as big as it was, I'd been bound to run into Cal. And even if I hadn't, there were reminders of him everywhere.

I thought I was stronger. I knew I hadn't moved on. But I wasn't waiting it out for him. I simply didn't want any man.

Bzzz. Bzzz. Bzzz.

A key to honing my strengths was recognizing my weakness. And talking to Cal . . . having anything to do with him was a giant mistake.

Pick up the phone.

I wanted to. I could almost feel the words as if he'd spoken them in that voice of his. It always had a depth, but it was the command. As if it were impossible to argue with him.

I will find you.
Don't make me come see for myself how you are.

There wasn't any sexual innuendo or promise. It was straight-up concern. And I didn't have room in my life for that.

My hand trembled as it hovered over the screen. I stared at it. I should say this in person. Or at the very least over the phone, so he could hear I meant it. I held my breath as I used one thumb to type.

This is done.

Why did I suddenly feel so . . . hollow? No. *It's done.* That was the right choice. And yet, I felt so wrong inside. I was supposed to walk away and feel victory. Like I'd finally settled the score.

I waited for the triumph to wash over me. But it never came.

Those blasted three dots blinked. And blinked. And blinked.

Was he going to respond? Or had he left the app open and forgotten about me already? Just like he had all those years ago.

Forget him. You have bigger problems to think about.

But Cal wouldn't get out of my head. Not the way I felt protected when he held me. Or cared for when he looked at me with one of those soul-deep stares. Or the jolt of excitement every time his name lit my screen.

Somehow my anger and hurt only intensified it all.

Bzzz.

I couldn't look at the screen. I wasn't ready for a response, whatever it may be. Because like always, I had no idea what was coming next when it came to Garrett Calhoun.

The phone vibrated again in my hand, a second notification of my unread text message.

My stomach dropped when I read the words.

I'm on my way.

CHAPTER SIXTEEN

CAL

WHAT ARE YOU DOING?

Teague had mentioned in passing a while back that she was staying with Lincoln while she was in town. I wasn't exactly sure what building it was, though I knew it was somewhere around the park.

It wouldn't be hard to find the address.

You got no business crossing over into that world.

She'd made it my business when she'd shut me out... over a text.

Oh no, baby sister. This ain't done by a long shot.

I hesitated with my keys in my fist. She'd given me the out I needed. This time she'd been the one to walk away. This tryst had an expiration date. Always had, considering she lived an ocean away.

Even if she lived over by the park permanently, the distance might as well have been the same as London. It was a different world. One I didn't belong in.

She wanted this thing over? I should let her have her way.

But I wasn't done.

I had eleven years to make up for.

This is done.

What I had realized when I read those three catastrophic words was that I only had a small blip of time to get my fill for the next decade ... or more.

I hadn't yet.

My phone rang. B flashed across the screen. I couldn't put in her full name in case one of the nosy guys at the station snooped through my phone. Her name was too unique. They'd know it was Hollingsworth's sister. And that I had no good reason to have her number.

"You can't stop me."

I shoved my wallet in my back pocket.

"No." The one word was a sharp stab. "You can't come here. If someone sees you..."

Stab. Stab. Stab.

"Answer my question and then you won't have to worry about getting caught with the wrong kinda man," I said through my teeth.

Her dirty little secret.

That was all I'd ever been. All I could be.

"I did." Her smoky voice rose. "I told you it felt like my hand—"

"Had been put through a meat grinder." I remembered every word she said. "And it'll feel worse tomorrow because you aren't taking care of it."

"What difference does it make to you?"

Good question.

I didn't know the answer. Only that it did.

"Where's your brother's apartment?" *Are you out of your ever-loving mind? You have no good reason to show up there. No explanation. And when Teague finds out, he'll kill you.*

"How do you know that?" Her tone had lost the feistiness and turned straight up cold ... with fear?

I wanted to do a lot of things to Beau, but scare her wasn't one of them.

"Teague mentioned it," I grunted.

Hang up the phone. Let her have her way.

"What a blabbermouth," she muttered, but as long as that fear was gone, I'd take it.

Who scares you, Beau?

She was fearless. Always unafraid. Maybe that was why she'd snuck around with me before. To live on the edge. To be somewhere she wasn't supposed to be.

The woman was a lot of things, but scared wasn't one of them. And hearing that little hint of fear sent a streak of unsettledness through me.

Water sloshing came through the phone from the other end.

"Where are you?"

"Our arrangement doesn't include conversation."

Stab.

Because my body was good enough for her to use, but the rest of me wasn't. *Get over yourself, Cal.* It wasn't like I'd exactly been a wordsmith around her either. Unless "take your clothes off" counted.

"Arrangement? As in present tense?" I so wished I could see her face. "We're not done yet, Beau."

More water splashed.

"We're done when I say we are."

I laughed, though it was hollow. "You think you control this?"

Even I wasn't foolish enough to believe I did either. If I did, I'd be channel surfing, pretending I'd only heard her name in the paper . . . which I didn't read. Instead, it had taken one look for me to get sucked right back into her orbit.

I knew better.

It hadn't ended well before, and we were headed for disaster again. But I couldn't predict the collision date. The only thing I could do was buckle up and enjoy the ride before it killed me.

"Don't tell me you think you do."

It was a taunt, meant to insult, but that wouldn't work when I'd already faced the truth.

"No. I sure as hell don't."

A long silence fell between us.

Hang up the damn phone.

Instead, I cradled it between my ear and shoulder and sat back on my couch.

"Why did you text me? After Cassano's funeral?"

There was no fire behind the questions. No bite or zip. None of her usual attitude toward me.

I'd asked myself the same thing no less than a thousand times over the past few weeks. The answer still evaded me.

"I don't know." I hated the way those words sounded coming out of my mouth.

"Still honest to a fault." She snorted bitterly. "I'm glad to know it wasn't my irresistible pull. Or even that you'd hit a dry spell and were just hard up."

There it was. That rare glimpse at her vulnerability.

Beau was the most confident person I'd ever known. She carried herself with authority and grace. She was indestructible. Nothing swayed her. She didn't need anyone.

A few times she'd given me a peek beneath her outer walls. Something I didn't think she did very often and probably hated doing now. It drew me further into her web.

And honest to a fault?

No way would I admit she'd figured out the answer even when I hadn't.

She *did* have a pull on me I couldn't explain or fight against. I'd done it successfully once and it had taken everything I had.

"I don't need to be hard up to want you."

That was *not* what was supposed to come out of my mouth. She was right. We needed to go back to less talking.

"I just wanted a hot bath." She sounded far away, like she was talking to herself instead of me. And she was exhausted.

That explained all the sloshing around.

"Teague's calling. I have to go," she said.

"I'll wait."

You really and truly have lost your mind. It had been the excuse I needed to put distance between us. And when the opportunity presented itself, I didn't want it.

I twirled my keyring around my finger. I hated days off. A restlessness that never seemed to go away ate at me.

After I'd left Ma's, I'd gone over to what was left of Joe's place. I'd seen more burned buildings than the average person, but it had still been a shock. We'd been there only hours before, getting his stuff. Now he had nothing left but the bag he'd brought to my place.

I'd dropped by the station to see him. His state was mostly unchanged. He wouldn't say more than a few words, except he had to work overnight. It was a lie. He didn't have to. He wanted to. Because it was where he felt most comfortable. I didn't begrudge him that.

More water came through the line, except it sounded like a tub draining.

"I really have to go. There's a rescue a couple hours away and they need me to watch the dogs." She was more alert, back to business.

"You can't watch that many dogs with your hand like that."

"*Goodbye, Cal.*"

I checked the screen. She'd hung up on me again.

Twice in one night? I didn't think so.

Little miss thought she could get rid of me that easy? I had news for her.

It wasn't happening.

CHAPTER SEVENTEEN

BEAU

HE WAS RIGHT.

I made a noise of frustration at the unwanted thought. My hand hurt and I'd only let one dog out of his kennel, a sweet one named Lucky. He was gentle, even if he'd jumped a little when I'd let him out first. But looping a leash around his neck one-handed? I just hoped they didn't have a security camera.

I surveyed the line of kennels. There were a lot of dogs to walk. Like twelve at least. And I'd have to do it one at a time.

I'd had a little practice with Muffy and Millie, but this was a monumental task. I honestly had no idea how Pepper, Miss Adeline, and Teague did it.

"At least you've been fed," I said under my breath. I scratched behind Lucky's ears. "Go easy on me?"

He licked at my hand, and I patted his head.

"Okay, troops. We'll be back in a bit."

A few of the dogs barked in response, though one seemed to be giving me the stink eye. *Sadie.*

How could I forget she did everything first?

"Not tonight, sweetheart." I'd already leashed up Lucky and wasn't about to undo it.

I touched his nose. "Ready?"

He stamped his feet in approval, and I smiled, temporarily forgetting everything but the dogs. It was nice to have something else to focus on.

I waved to the doorman as we exited the building onto the sidewalk. It was still hard to believe the old Grey Paws location in Chelsea had burned. Thank goodness Daniel Elliott had so generously given them a place to go.

"Good evening, miss," he said kindly.

Lucky sniffed his pocket, then pranced past when there was nothing of interest in it. He went to the left as if he knew where he was headed, and I was more than happy to let him lead.

"Are you determined not to heal?"

I jolted at Cal's voice from behind. Lucky took that as a sign to go faster. The greyhound bolted to the corner, dragging me behind like a rag doll. Thank God I had on flats. It was all I could do to keep upright.

"Lucky!"

He stopped before the street and sat, looking up at me with big eyes. His tongue was out, but he wasn't panting.

Meanwhile, my arm felt like it had been pulled out of the socket and I could hardly breathe. *If I'd have lost this dog, I'd never forgive myself.*

Cal grabbed the leash.

"I've got it," I said, refusing to let go.

"Looks like it." He kept his grip firm around the rope.

Lucky looked back and forth between us, uncertain.

"You're scaring him."

"Give me the damn leash before you break your neck."

"What are you doing here anyway?"

He pulled. "Helping a friend."

"I'm not your friend."

"I was talking about Teague."

Had my brother called him too? Maybe I didn't have much experience with dogs, but he could count on me. It hurt a little if he thought I needed backup.

"Right now, you're not helping." I tightened my grip on the leash.

"Because you're being stubborn." He pried my fingers loose. "I swear you have the will of a bull."

"And you have the temperament of one," I muttered, annoyed he now held the leash.

Instead of taking off with Lucky, he reached for my hand. It was dark, but he held it up to a streetlight with the gentlest of touches. "Still swollen," he said more to himself than to me.

Eleven years ago, this man had cast me aside like I'd meant nothing to him. I'd never really known what heartbreak felt like until that moment. But being spurned and told we were just temporary fun had shattered me. Perhaps it had eventually also made me stronger. More resilient. But I'd never forgotten his words, nor the pain I'd lived with for months afterward. And yet, now, as if he felt he still had the right —as if I meant something to him—he acted like it was the end of the world because I had an injured hand. Those two things didn't mesh.

It was a lot easier to keep control when he was only using me for something physical just the way I was him. And physical didn't include tender touches.

Lucky stamped his paws with a look like *are we walking or not?*

Cal released me with a dissatisfied grunt. "Are you up for this?"

"We're walking a dog, not climbing Mount Everest." I pressed my fingers to my forehead. At least he'd asked. Everyone else seemed to dictate my every move. "Let's go," I said with a less acidic tone.

Lucky popped up and looked both ways down the street. How did he know to do that?

The crosswalk sign lit green, and he trotted off at an easy pace toward the park across the street.

"I can't believe your brother was going to let you be out here on your own at night," Cal said as we wandered behind Lucky.

"Unlike you, he knows I can handle myself." And he was desperate. But I wasn't going to mention that. Because under normal circumstances, he'd have made sure someone else was with me. I narrowed my gaze. "Wait a minute. He didn't call you to help too?"

Cal looked at me with a cool expression that gave nothing away.

Lucky found a tree and marked it as his own. Then he claimed a bench and a bush too.

"Hello. I asked you a question," I finally said when he didn't reply.

"I'm here. Does it matter why?" He steered Lucky away from a little dog who yapped at him.

The sweet boy was a giant compared to the other dog, but was frightened. He jumped away and tucked his tail.

Cal squatted so that Lucky was cocooned between his strong thighs. "It's just a little rat," he said softly, rubbing up and down his sides. "You could eat it as a snack."

It was a ridiculous thought, but the soothing tone he used made it sound not so bad. Lucky inched toward him and licked his face. His tail even wiggled a little.

The man and his dog kept moving until they were no longer visible.

Cal cradled Lucky's face and rubbed his thumbs over his head. "They're gone. You're okay."

And just like that, he'd knocked a fissure in the wall I had around me to protect myself from him.

He stood and readjusted the leash. "We'd better go back or your friends will be mad you hogged all the walking time."

He headed back in the direction of Grey Paws. I remained frozen. Cal and a dog. How was I supposed to resist that?

Cal glanced over his shoulder. "You coming?"

Damn it. I wasn't supposed to see him outside of bedrooms. I wasn't supposed to have conversation with him. And I wasn't supposed to get a little weak-kneed from watching him comfort a scared dog.

Find your steel, Beau. You're going to need it.

I quickened my pace. "I'm coming."

CHAPTER EIGHTEEN

CAL

THREE HOURS.

That was how long it had taken to walk thirteen dogs. I had a new respect for animal rescues. How was Teague doing this and keeping up at the station?

I wanted a distraction.

Pretending to make a social call to my friend just so I could see Beau had proven to be more of one than I expected.

"I think that's the last one." Beau collapsed in a chair and put her feet on the table.

I unlatched each kennel and let the dogs come out if they wanted. Teague had called as we were finishing up the walks. They were on their way back, but it would be a few hours. I'd promised we wouldn't leave until they returned.

"Want a beer?" I opened the fridge where I'd been assured there were some and found a six-pack.

"Please."

Beau dropped her head back. I hadn't seen her this relaxed since we were kids. She always had this put together air around others, but back then, when she was with me, she let loose.

"You eaten?"

Ma had fed me the equivalent of a Thanksgiving meal for lunch, but that was long gone.

"No." She accepted the beer I offered.

"Other hand."

She glared, but her injury could still use something cold on it. I took a swig, and she made an exaggerated motion of doing the same, making sure *not* to do as I'd said.

I flipped through my phone and found the number for Dino's. They should still be open if we hurried. "Pizza? Or is that not frou-frou enough for you?"

"Only vegetable."

I groaned as I dialed. "You used to eat meat."

She flinched. "I still do."

Instead of what I usually would have ordered—a pizza with no vegetables—I heard myself ask for what Beau wanted.

I'd be starving again in a few hours but didn't want an argument.

"It'll be here in half an hour." I tossed my phone on the table.

We were surrounded by greyhounds. Most of them had found a bed to pass out on. Two were at my feet with their heads on top of them.

Some of them had been a little rowdy, but overall, well-behaved. Better than I expected. Who knew what these dogs had been through?

Lucky put his head in my lap and let out a sigh.

A dog might be good for Ma.

One would be good company and maybe she'd get a little exercise. I could talk to Teague about it. Hell, Ma might like to come visit the dogs here. We'd never had one growing up, so I wasn't sure she was into them.

For that matter, Bobby's and Mike's kids would like a couple of these guys. It might help Joe too.

Who did I think I was? The dog fairy?

Although this had made me understand Teague a bit better. It had surprised me and the guys how much time he'd given Pepper, Miss Adeline, and Grey Paws, but I was starting to get it. These dogs gave back. We gave a lot of ourselves every shift at work, but these dogs gave something back. Unconditionally.

"Did you ever have a dog?" I swallowed a long pull of beer.

Her gold earrings caught in the light. I'd buried my face in that spot behind her ear so many times it felt like home. The skin was soft and faintly tan and smelled so good it made me crazy.

She made me crazy.

"I'm not doing this with you."

I set my beer down. "It's just a question. What do you think is gonna happen if you answer it?"

I was the one who had more at stake if she did. The more she offered of herself, the more I had to let go of when the time came.

She traced the rim of the bottle, then looked at me with bitterness. "Like my father would ever have allowed a dog in his house."

The image of a sad and lonely little girl isolated in her father's kingdom flashed in my head. She'd never talked much about him. Her brothers, on the other hand, she'd chattered away about. But they were a few years older. There had to have been a point when she'd been alone.

And I didn't like that.

"Did you want one?"

The hint of a smile ghosted her lips. "At one point I wanted a zoo."

I lifted a brow.

"I mean I literally wanted my father to buy me a zoo."

I could easily picture Beau demanding what she wanted from her father. At the same time, I couldn't imagine her ever asking anyone for anything. If she wanted a zoo, she'd figure out the way to get it herself.

"I take it that didn't go over well."

Her mouth flattened and she cut her eyes to the side. "I got a trip to the zoo with my grandmother. She wouldn't let me feed the camel. It was not a good day."

"How old were you?"

"Seven." She made another face. "I'm pretty sure my father took after her. She wouldn't even let me have ice cream." She lifted a shoulder and lowered it. "What grandmother doesn't let her granddaughter have ice cream?"

"Lactose intolerant ones?"

It was completely inappropriate. Beau was opening up to me in a way she hadn't ever before. The day had obviously been a bit traumatic and I'd made light of it.

She sprayed beer all over the table when she laughed.

I hadn't heard that sound in years. It was more beautiful now with age and experience. Like it wasn't freely given. And I wanted to hear it again.

A couple of the dogs lifted their heads, but when everything appeared okay, they put them back down.

"Grandmothers or grandkids?" She snickered.

I leaned back in my chair. "Both?"

"Maybe that was her problem."

"Ma took us to the zoo once."

"Only once?"

"She had six boys. Ben climbed into the bear exhibit—"

"He what?" Her eyes went wide. "I thought they had glass."

"Not back then." A laugh threatened to escape. "You should've seen him when that bear started coming toward him." I couldn't stop the laugh. "He-he climbed that fence again so fast—"

I couldn't finish the sentence, too choked up with laughter just thinking about it.

"He could've been hurt," Beau said, but her lips twitched.

"Yeah, but Ma was screaming so loud that the bear was terrified." I covered my mouth. The scene had been pure chaos. And me and my brothers had been rolling on the ground it was so funny. Except Ben.

"I bet she was scared too."

"She was pissed." I petted Lucky's head. "She wasn't screaming at the bear. She was screaming at my brother."

And then it broke free. Another laugh. This one was better than the first she'd let go.

"Are you serious?" She looked at me as if she weren't sure.

I put my hand on my heart. "I swear on Pop's grave."

Her bright expression turned to one of sympathy. "I'm sorry about your dad."

The stab of sensation her laugh had caused in my chest was different than this one. This slash hurt as fresh as the day he'd been killed.

I flicked my chin in acknowledgment. There was nothing to say. He wasn't coming back. Maybe one day the pain would subside to a dull ache.

"I should've—"

"Nah." I shook my head. "There was nothing you could've done. I didn't deserve it anyway."

She looked down in quiet acceptance. "Were you there?"

I swallowed as if the thick smoke filled the room all over again. "I carried him out of the building." I could feel the weight of him in my arms. The fear and adrenaline as I fought my way out of the flames. "He was already gone."

I'd refused to accept the truth even as they'd put him in the ambulance. I had barely been able to face my brothers, knowing I hadn't done enough to save him. I'd dreaded the moment I'd had to tell Ma that Pop wasn't coming home.

But it had been my responsibility to break the news to her. Even now, the lead of my footsteps as I'd gone up the front walk and the pit in my stomach was as fresh as it had been then. She'd crumpled in my arms, beat my chest, and screamed that I was a liar. Something I recalled in every nightmare I had of that night. The worst day of my life.

I'd held her for three hours while she'd cried, my guilt only growing stronger with every passing minute.

I drained the rest of my beer and set the empty bottle on the table a little too loudly. It was the stuff of nightmares. I couldn't stand to think about it. Refused to now.

I stalked around the table to her side. It creaked when I rested against it. I took the bottle from her hands and blindly set it beside me.

I'd disturbed the dogs again, if only temporarily, but they settled quickly.

Beau's expression turned guarded, wary. It should be. I didn't know what I was going to do next either. Only that a table distance apart had been too far.

I lifted my arm.

"There might be cameras," she said quietly.

I dropped it and turned my head away. "Shit."

For a minute, I'd forgotten about being her secret. If Teague found out, he'd kill me in a slow, torturous death . . . just as I would him if the roles were reversed.

Discreetly, she nudged my foot with hers. I forced myself to look at her. And I didn't like what I saw.

She was a reminder of the untouchable thing I'd held for a moment, but couldn't keep. A sucker punch to the face of mistakes I couldn't fix. How doing the right thing felt so wrong. And the wrong thing . . . I wanted a whole lot more of that.

When she'd said we were done earlier tonight, I should've let her walk like she wanted to.

But I couldn't. Not yet. Especially after sharing a few uncomplicated hours. Where we'd almost felt like friends. Like we'd been years ago. Whether either of us liked it, we weren't done. Not by a long shot.

CHAPTER NINETEEN

BEAU

"PUPPIES?"

I peered into the giant basket Teague held where tiny little faces were sleeping peacefully. Like they knew they were safe.

"Six," he said in a hushed tone as he set the basket on the table. "I've seen a lot of awful stuff over my career, but this . . ." He shuddered. "My eyes have been opened since I started rescuing dogs with Pepper."

My brother's fiancée was pulled over by a giant greyhound, who wasn't satisfied until she reached her puppies. She was thin, unbearably so, but clearly feisty when it came to these puppies. She stretched her neck to see in the basket and barked when she couldn't.

Teague pulled two chairs together and moved it to the seats. She sniffed, checking them out until she was satisfied.

"You're such a good mama, Copper." Pepper rubbed her head. The dog looked at her like she was uncertain what Pepper was doing. "You and your babies are going to be fine now."

Woof.

I jerked my head toward Miss Adeline who held an even larger, yet equally thin, dog on a leash.

"Another one?" I asked incredulously. They'd nearly doubled the number of dogs they had in a single night.

"We think this is the papa," Miss Adeline said. "In all my years, I've never seen a dog so protective of his family."

He pulled her toward Copper and the puppies.

"What happens now?" I dropped to my knees next to them.

The male jumped away, though he kept between me and the others.

Cal stepped between me and them. Teague, Pepper, and Miss Adeline all looked at him curiously. He said nothing, just watched the dog carefully.

I had an up-close view of his ass.

"We bathe them, find a place where they can be together, and nurse them back to health." There was no hesitation in Pepper's plan of action. She was confident these dogs would be all right.

I admired her positivity. She made me believe that they would make a full recovery and the puppies would grow to have an amazing life.

"You better put those puppies close to where you bathe that one or it ain't happening." Cal pointed at the male.

"I hate to ask you for anything else," Pepper said apologetically. "But would you mind helping us do that? We could use another set of strong hands."

"Whatever you need," he said, voice gruff.

Teague punched him in the arm. "You may regret those words."

Copper circled the basket, sniffing. Her nose worked its way over to Cal. She smelled his shoe, then his shin, then his knee. And then she sat, leaning against his leg.

She poked her head through them, staring at me.

"Hi, Copper," I said gently.

She blinked.

"I bet you'll feel better after a bath. Or are you hungry?"

Sadie sat up from a dead sleep and barked.

"Um, Beau. There are certain words we have to use sparingly around here." Teague pointed his head toward the dog.

I guessed hungry was one of them.

Pepper tossed Sadie a treat. She gobbled it up and passed out again.

Copper watched the whole thing as if she'd never seen anything like it before.

"We've walked them, so you can take the leash off her," Pepper said as she moved toward the kitchen area.

I reached through Cal's legs at the same time he moved to remove Copper's leash. Our fingers brushed, and it was like a jolt of electricity. I'd deluded myself into thinking he only affected me because it was straight up physical.

And not that there was ever a time I wasn't attracted to him, but now wasn't sexual. We were here to help people we cared about. I wasn't thinking about him *that* way.

And I hated how potent his touch was.

I yanked my hand back to my lap like I'd been burned. Cal continued on with the task easily, as if he hadn't noticed we'd touched. He set the leash on the table.

"Would you mind giving this to her?" Pepper handed him a small bowl of food.

He took it, looking uncertain, but bent to set it on the floor. Copper sniffed the contents, then turned her head away.

"Sometimes we have to hand feed them," Teague said.

Cal sat on the floor beside me. The male dog edged closer, and my heart twisted. He wasn't sure we weren't going to hurt her.

What had they been through?

And how brave these dogs were.

Cal scooped a little of the food on his finger. He held it out. Both dogs sniffed, tempted yet still unsure.

And Cal let them take their time. He didn't say words to coax them or shove his finger closer. He allowed them to do it at their own pace.

Copper slid to her belly as if she didn't have any more energy.

I touched her back, and she flinched.

"I'm sorry, sweetheart," I said softly. "You'll learn we don't want to hurt you."

She inched closer to Cal.

"Does he have a name?" I asked, discreetly pointing at the daddy dog.

"Brutus." Miss Adeline smirked. "Doesn't that just fit him perfectly?"

"At least you didn't name him after the fireman on the calendar," Pepper said as she gathered supplies to feed the puppies.

"Ooh. Good idea. That's twelve names we don't have to think of."

"You are *not* naming a dog after me," Teague said.

Pepper smiled mischievously. "I don't know . . . it kind of has a nice ring to it."

He put a hand to his forehead. "I can't win with these two."

Miss Adeline touched Cal's shoulder. "I'm glad you're back in this year. I missed seeing you for a while."

He blushed. Had I ever seen him do that?

"*Woman.*" Pepper's face was red too. "You're going to run off everyone if you keep flirting with them."

"Since when is telling the truth flirting?" she asked innocently.

"Hey." Teague narrowed his gaze, looking suspiciously at Cal and me. "Did you two patch things up? You're not arguing. Or glaring." He tilted his head. "What's that all about anyway?"

A knot formed in my stomach. "There was nothing to patch up." Did I sound cool and detached? I hoped so.

Miss Adeline nudged Teague. "How do you usually work out your tension with Pepper?"

Realization dawned on his features. Then he was glaring at Cal. "You better not be 'working' anything out that way with my sister." He stepped between us. "In fact, you're too close to her now."

"*Teague.*" It was my turn for the hot cheeks. "I'm not twelve. And nobody is working anything out."

He pointed at me. "Maybe you need to move in with us where I can keep an eye on you. Lincoln's been preoccupied."

"Oh don't worry. He's inserted himself quite well in my comings and goings," I said, voice rising.

"Chill, Hollingsworth. You really think your sister would be interested in the likes of me?"

I frowned at Cal. He'd made the comment offhandedly to get Teague off our case. But something about it bothered me. *Did he really believe that?* Because in my gut, I felt he wasn't referring to the ugly end we'd had all those years ago. *That* most definitely was a reason to steer clear of him.

The idea that I thought I was better than him . . . on what basis? Had I behaved that way?

I hated him because of what he'd done, not who he was. Our difference in upbringing didn't matter to me. Other than my brothers, I'd have traded places with him in a heartbeat. He was far wealthier in the ways that mattered than I was.

"WE'RE ALMOST OUT OF GAS."

He banged the steering wheel.

I reached in my purse and fished out a twenty. "Stop at the next station."

He glared at the bill I'd stuffed in the ashtray. "I don't need your money."

"You always pay. It's my turn," *I said, trying to make light. It was twenty bucks. No big deal.*

"You don't have a turn when it comes to that," *he said through his teeth as he wheeled up to a gas pump.*

"It's not all on you—"

He slammed the door and shut down that thought. With long, powerful strides, he strode into the convenience store.

We'd been having a good time just cruising around the city. At least I had been. One mention of money and he'd turned into a hothead. Who happened to look unbelievably handsome when he was mad.

I didn't want to ruin our day over something stupid.

He stalked back to the truck and started the gas pump.

I opened my door and swung so I was facing out. "I have two favorite places."

He stared at the numbers on the pump, jaw tight . . . ignoring me.

"Since you asked," *I continued, my heart beating a little faster.* "The roof. And your truck."

He swung his eyes toward me.

"You don't have to be so thrilled." I pinched his cheek.

The pump clicked off. Five dollars. That was all he'd gotten. Was that even enough to take me back to Manhattan?

Why did he have to be so stubborn? I could fix this. A tank of gas wasn't a million dollars.

I stuffed my rising irritation down. Teague and Lincoln had taught me awareness of how people reacted to money by their example. Neither of them treated anyone any differently, no matter where they came from. They never flaunted our trusts.

Teague hid the fact he had one from most of his friends.

I wouldn't let something so unimportant be a wedge between Garrett and me.

"Just because you ignore me doesn't mean I'm not here." I caught his hand and tugged.

Eventually he stepped between my legs. He hadn't let go of my hand. That had to be a good sign, didn't it?

"You think I can forget about you?" His breath was warm with a hint of wintergreen. He inched closer until his lips were a whisper away from mine. "There's not a second of the day you're not on my mind. And there never will be."

My lungs seized. They were just words. But *he'd* said them. And I believed him.

I brushed my lips across his.

Promises. I didn't want them from just anyone. I wanted them from him. Because whether he realized it or not, I'd made one to him too.

He had my heart.

The most important thing I had to give. And it was his. Completely.

"Don't start something I'll finish right here," he warned huskily as I rubbed my heel down the back of his thigh.

"Would I do something like that?" I touched my chest.

A corner of his mouth loosened. The storm clouds had parted in his eyes. "Yes."

He brusquely kissed me. "Shit. There's Burke. And Teague."

Panic shot through me. I dove for the backseat. Please don't let them see us.

I lay on the floorboard and pulled a jacket and a blanket over me.
Someday you have to tell Teague.
I knew that. But today was not that day.

YOU HID HIM.

Not because I was ashamed. If my father had found out about us, I'd have never seen Garrett again. And clearly Teague would've murdered him for touching me.

I was protecting him.

Were you?

Yes. Back then anyway. Now I had no reason to. There was simply no point in stirring up a hornet's nest over something temporary.

I reached out to Brutus without thought, petting his head. Cal had lied. And the twenty-something I'd once been had believed him.

It wasn't him who never stopped thinking of me.

I glared at him as the ugly realization hit me.

I had never stopped thinking about him.

CHAPTER TWENTY

CAL

"JUST CRASH HERE."

Tempting as it was, I shook my head. "Thanks for the offer, but I got a ton of stuff to do before my shift tomorrow."

And I couldn't risk spending the night with Beau only a room away. She'd been frigid since they'd arrived back with the new dogs. But there wasn't a cold wind coming from her direction. She'd shut the door so there was nothing.

Like I was nothing.

"We really appreciate you looking out for our furry monsters." Pepper tucked herself against Teague's side.

"Glad to help," I brushed off the gratitude. He'd have done the same for me if I'd asked.

"I know you're busy, but Copper seems to feel safe around you." Pepper worried her lip. "Could you come by? Just when you have time. It might help her adjust more quickly."

I glanced to the dog asleep next to her puppies in a makeshift pen we'd put together.

"Sure."

"Do you need me anymore?" Beau put a hand on her purse strap.

"So you're not going to stay either?" Teague kissed the side of Pepper's head. "I'll take you home."

"How much longer are you here?" Pepper asked.

Beau shifted uncomfortably. "I'm . . . not sure."

"If you don't mind an old lady and some dogs, we'd love to have you spend a few days with us before you go," she said. "You'll be here for the wedding, right?"

Beau's features softened. "I wouldn't miss it. And I don't mind old ladies, dogs, or overbearing brothers."

Teague dug in his pockets and pulled out his keys. "I'm not overbearing," he grumbled. "You ready?"

"I'll drive you." The words were out of my mouth before I could stop them.

"Can you two stand to be in a confined space for that long?" Teague raised a brow.

"It's only twenty minutes tops, right?" I pretended it wasn't a big deal.

But it was.

She hadn't been in my truck in a long time. I doubted it was one of her favorite places anymore.

"I'll take a cab."

"No."

"No."

Teague and I spoke simultaneously.

Beau scowled.

Pepper ducked out from under Teague's arm. "I think I'm going to skip this argument. Save yourself the trouble, Beau, and just ride home with Cal."

"Fine." She kissed her brother's cheek and then Pepper's. "Love you."

A pit formed in my stomach. She used to say that to me.

I slapped Teague's hand in a bro handshake and hugged Pepper. "See you. And give Miss Adeline—"

"I'll tell her you said bye. I'm not giving her anything for you."

Pepper put a hand to her head. "I don't want to start something." Then she grinned.

"Fair enough." I flicked my chin at Beau. "I'm parked a few blocks away."

Without a word, we walked to my truck. Every step closer, my anxiety ratcheted up another notch. It was one thing to spend a few hours with her in a random hotel room and completely different to go back to a place that had meant something to both of us. Had been "our place."

I had no illusions about what had been going on between us since she'd been back. Had no illusions things would be different this time. But the more distance we kept, the less personal, the easier it would be when we had to part ways.

What's more personal than being inside of her?

Being with her in that truck. Our physical relationship had always been just one form of our communication. It was raw and deep and unfiltered. As intimate and sacred as it was, sharing what was in my head was more so.

I'd opened up to her in ways I never had to anyone. My family knew me through and through . . . but not the way Beau did.

And most of my confessions had come in the truck or on the roof.

Maybe if I didn't speak, I could make it. Like I'd told Teague . . . it was only twenty minutes.

I unlocked the passenger side door and held it open for her. She climbed in like she'd never stopped.

Stab.

How could a woman getting in my truck cause that reaction?

I secured her inside and rounded the hood. A black car was parked across the street, the engine quietly running. The windows were too dark to tell if someone was inside.

This was New York. People were out at all hours. Including us.

I cranked the ignition and immediately turned down the radio when a few notes of "Wild Horses" by The Rolling Stones came through the speakers. She didn't need to hear my walk down memory lane and I wasn't in the mood to make mine any worse.

I checked the rearview and pulled into the street. She sat stiffly with her hands in her lap. That was different. Before, she'd always been relaxed in that seat.

The late hour meant traffic was fairly light.

"Where am I headed?"

My voice was rough, like I hadn't used it in days. Like she affected me.

"Park." She was still cold and distant. "I'll tell you where to turn."

I drummed my fingers on the steering wheel. The silence closed in around us. There was a time it would've been comfortable. Now, it felt like it was squeezing the life out of me.

I cracked the window, hoping some fresh air would clear my lungs. It didn't.

I'd been with her in confined spaces over the past few weeks. That motel we'd gone to the most had tiny rooms. But it hadn't been like this.

She turned up the radio and the song had changed to "I'm On Fire" by Bruce Springsteen. It might as well have been a hand tightening around my throat.

We'd driven these very streets with that song on repeat. She'd made an entire tape of just that song. It was in the glovebox.

"Is this on the radio?"

There was a touch of hope in her voice. Hope that this was just a random blast from the past.

"No." I turned my head slightly, trying to suck in more fresh air.

She stared at the dash where it dimly glowed. "A tape?" The question was a croak.

Finally.

An indication that it wasn't just me who was affected.

I ejected it, held it up so she could see the faded Sharpie on the label.

Her handwriting.

Driving music.

With a heart beside the letters.

I popped it back into the tape deck and music overtook the quiet again. Maybe the song was worse than the silence.

"I'm taking that," she said quietly.

"I don't think so, baby sister. You gave that to me." *And it's all I have left of you.* "Unless you're wanting to take a walk down memory lane."

"No." She fidgeted with the long gold chain around her neck.

Good.

I hoped she was as uncomfortable as I was.

This ride was your idea, jackass.

And it was the worst one I'd had in a long time.

"I can't believe that dog likes you," she muttered.

"There was a time when you did too."

She edged closer to the door at the reminder. Like if she could get farther away from me, I'd disappear.

"I suppose I owe you a debt of gratitude," she said bitterly. "Because of you I learned not to trust so easily. I've never made that mistake again."

How could words be a stab to the chest and a relief at the same time? I probably was just hearing what I wanted to, but I took them to mean she hadn't had a relationship with anyone after me.

I was supposed to have wanted her to move on, to be happy. My grip was so tight on the steering wheel that pain shot through my knuckles. I didn't want her with anyone else.

But she wasn't mine to have anymore.

I checked the rearview. *Is that the car that had been parked near Teague's?* It was hard to tell with the headlights shining in my eyes.

I put on a signal and changed lanes. The car was a respectable distance back, but after a few seconds, made the same move. I drove a few more blocks and switched lanes again.

The car followed.

"What are you doing?" Beau asked. "You missed the turn."

"I thought you were going to give me directions." I checked the mirror every few seconds.

"And I thought you knew how to get to Park Avenue."

"We're taking a detour." Abruptly, I spun the wheel to take the next street.

She grasped for the door, trying to find something to hold on to. "Are you trying to wreck?"

"Nope."

The car made the turn behind us. I sped up and took another street.

"I should've had Teague take me home. At least I'd make it in one piece." She was halfway over the console as I took another turn.

A whiff of her scent overpowered the fresh air flowing through the open window. *Damn it. Why does that get me every time?*

I needed to concentrate. Because the car hung right with us, keeping enough distance to make me question if I was crazy.

The tires squealed as I wheeled onto another street.

"Cal. What are you doing?"

My jaw worked. "Don't call me Cal."

I hated it. Hated it on her lips anyway.

"Everyone else does."

"And you ain't everyone else."

She pulled on the door handle. "Let me out. I'll take a cab."

"No."

"You're driving like a maniac."

"You were never scared in the car with me before."

Turn.

Another turn.

Turn again.

I couldn't shake the car.

"You were never this erratic."

"Would somebody want to follow you?" I asked through my teeth. Because I couldn't think of a single person who would have a reason to tail me.

She twisted in her seat, looking out the back window. After a minute, she faced forward again and hung her head. "Just take me to Lincoln's."

Defeat was in every syllable.

And that was worse than her sharp attitude toward me. I'd take the feisty Beau any day over this.

"Who is that?"

She sat with her shoulders rounded, still fiddling with her necklace. "I can't do this anymore."

She spoke so softly, I almost didn't hear her.

I touched her leg, torn between trying to lose whoever was following us and comforting her. Beau always won out.

She stiffened at the unwanted contact, but I needed it. Needed to feel her. Because my heart felt like it was about to beat out of my chest.

I slowed to a more reasonable speed. She was right. It wasn't worth the risk of an accident.

"Can't do what?"

"He follows me. Everywhere."

Rage like I'd never known boiled to the surface. Some asshole wouldn't leave her alone? I slowed further. I'd stop this truck and make sure he never bothered her again.

What kind of creep would stalk her?

God knew I'd wanted to but only to make sure she was okay. I wasn't some sick twisted bastard who couldn't let her go.

I pulled over.

Actually, I was. But I was going to end this right now for her.

I threw the truck in park.

"Cal?"

"He's not going to bother you ever again." I yanked on the door handle. It didn't give. Locked.

I pulled up the lock.

She clamped a hand on my thigh. "You can't stop him."

"The hell I can't."

"He'll destroy you."

"Not without a clear message to leave you alone first."

I opened the door, had one foot out.

"Garrett. Stop."

Something in her desperation gave me pause.

"Please. Keep going. Just take me home."

I sat, half in and half out. The car pulled over several spaces back. No one got out.

"I need a good reason to do that."

She squeezed her eyes as if in pain. And I inched closer to getting out. If I could stop her hurt, I didn't care who did what to me.

"It's my father."

CHAPTER TWENTY-ONE
BEAU

HE'D SEEN *Cal's truck.*

I rolled over. Who was I kidding? He already knew it. If not from me, then from following Teague.

But I'd always been careful to keep Cal off my father's radar.

After the way Cal had tried to lose him, I wouldn't be able to explain that away. Not like I could have if he'd just driven me home like a normal person. It was just Teague's friend giving me a lift.

I turned again, adjusting the pillow.

I was a grown woman at the helm of a multi-billion-dollar company. And my father dictated my life.

In London, it was easier to keep the illusion that *I* was in control. That my decisions were my own.

But they weren't. And they never had been.

Time was running out or Father wouldn't be the only one controlling my life. Alex Davenport would be too.

What if I went back to London?

I could leave now. Make them follow me if they wanted me to do as they said.

What about Teague and Pepper's wedding?

I promised I wouldn't miss it. I didn't want to miss it.

And it was another thing my father was trying to steal from me.

I threw the duvet off. Three in the morning. Sleep was a lost cause. My hand hurt. And if I had to be alone with my thoughts one more second, I'd go mad.

I wanted Cal. I wanted him to make me forget all of it.

"Argh." I switched on the bedside lamp.

No. I hated . . . I hated what he'd done. Hated how he made me feel. Hated that I needed him. But I didn't hate him anymore. How could I after he so fiercely defended me tonight?

It wasn't supposed to go that way.

It was only physical.

You think you are so tough, Beau. But you're a fool. Did you really believe you could let him touch you and come out unscathed?

Yes. Yes I had.

And then he'd opened up about his dad. For Cal to say anything was the equivalent of him spilling his guts. The man had meant everything to him. The hurt that radiated from him had done something to me. Made me feel something other than anger toward him.

"POP, *there's somebody I want you to meet.*"

Garrett slung an arm around me. I blinked in surprise at him and the older version who'd just stepped onto the rooftop.

"This is Beau."

The man grinned. "I wondered who'd been taking up so much of my son's time." He ate up the distance between us in a few long strides and held out a hand. "It's nice to meet you, Beau."

Slowly, I placed my hand in his. He gave it a squeeze. A fatherly one. Not that I knew what that was like from experience. The gesture felt warm and kind.

"Beau, this is my pop." There was so much pride in Garrett's voice. Respect. Love.

It was palpable.

"Lovely to meet you, Mr. Calhoun." There was a slight tremble to my words.

Garrett and I had been sneaking around so long. We had an understanding that it was better all-around to keep our relationship a secret.

He talked so much about his dad—his whole family, really—that something strange formed inside me. Garrett had introduced me to one of the most important people in his life.

We hadn't figured out a way to move forward, but if this didn't mean he wanted to, I had no idea what would.

"You must be a pretty special lady if he's shared this spot with you." He winked at his son.

My father had never done that to me.

Garrett squeezed my shoulder, a silent agreement.

"It's become one of my favorites." My cheeks got hot. I wasn't shy, but I was out of my element. What if his dad didn't like me?

"It's one of mine too." He clapped Garrett's shoulder. "Don't tell your mother I got to meet your girl first. I'll never hear the end of it," he said affectionately.

His girl.

We'd fit so naturally that I never thought about titles or status when it came to our relationship.

I like that.

His girl. It fit. Because I was.

And I meant so much that he'd introduced me to his father. What would it be like to be part of their family? Would they accept Teague and Lincoln too?

Garrett laughed. "I won't."

"I gotta get back to work." His father motioned his head toward the door. "Make sure you come by for dinner soon. I apologize in advance for all the hooligans also known as my sons." He threw his hands up, even as he grinned. "I tried. God knows I have."

In only a few minutes, this man had treated me more like a daughter than my own father had in my lifetime. How could I ever thank Garrett for the experience? One I thought I'd never have.

"I turned out pretty damn good." Garrett smirked.

Mr. Calhoun's expression turned serious. "You did, son. I'm real proud of you."

He stood a little taller at the praise but didn't say anything.

"Make sure my boy treats you right. If he doesn't, you come see me. I'll set him straight."

I HADN'T GONE to see Cal's father. I'd been too hurt.

But in that one meeting, I'd not only seen the love between father and son, I'd *felt* it.

For a moment, I'd been a little part of that. Because Cal had thought enough of me to introduce me to the man who meant most to him.

And then he'd lost him in a horrific tragedy.

I shouldn't feel sympathy toward Cal. But I wouldn't have wished that on him. I *didn't* wish that on him.

I'd never had and never would have that kind of relationship with my father. I didn't like that something that special had been ripped away from Cal, even though his dad died doing what he loved.

It was wrong that they'd lost their relationship while my strained one continued on.

If Father was gone, what would I feel?

He'd loomed over my life for so long, I wasn't fool enough to believe I wouldn't notice the absence. Relief. Freedom.

Wouldn't there be some part of me that couldn't function without his presence? It was a warped and twisted thought. I was my own woman, wasn't I?

My phone lit with an incoming call. Thank goodness, I was rescued from my treacherous thoughts.

"Hey, lady."

"I just realized it must be a godawful hour in the States," my friend Lawson said when I answered. "But you sound awake, so I don't feel that bad."

Half a laugh escaped. "Oh, I'm awake."

"Whew." She sounded as if she'd collapsed into a chair. "I haven't talked to you in weeks because I'm a terrible friend. Catch me up on everything."

"You spoke to Cagan."

I wasn't mad. Lawson and I had met through him. He'd been friends with her husband for years, and by extension Lawson after she and Stuart were married. She was from California so Cagan thought we'd get along. Which we did.

"I have," she said carefully. "But not about you. Other than he bumped into you in New York."

"For such a big city, it's a small town." I settled back under the duvet and propped against the headboard.

"The same could be said of London, I suppose."

"Tell me everything I've missed," I said. "Besides all of you."

As hectic as things had been, I hadn't had much time to dwell on the life I had across the Atlantic. I was absorbed with joy over finally getting to hang out with my brothers and friends, old and new, that I hadn't given my friends in London much thought.

I missed them.

"Honestly, nothing has changed. Annie's house is still a three-ring circus, Joss is determined to live like she's in her twenties instead of almost forty, and Cagan might as well not come to dinner parties because he spends the entire time on that stupid phone. It's literally attached to his hand."

The familiarity of what she described settled me. I could picture all of it in my mind. And even the hint of a smile broke free.

"By the way, it's your turn to have us over. I *guess* we can make other arrangements, but you're not getting out of it when you get back," she said playfully.

"Thank you for giving me a pass." The smile widened, and this normalcy felt so good.

"You're welcome." She was quiet for a minute. Out of our group of friends, she was the most serious. The one who all of us called when we needed advice or just a shoulder to lean on. Because she kept a level head and had a way of putting things in perspective.

"I've missed you," I blurted before I could think better of it. Maybe it was seeing Cagan the other day and now talking to Lawson, but I felt torn between two worlds.

I wanted to be here with my family. But I had a family there too.

"Missed you too. We all have. It's not the same without you here."

My chest squeezed. Before she'd called, hadn't I been ready to run back to London to escape my problems?

"I'm sure it's quite boring in my absence," I said, faking a posh voice.

"Quite." She laughed before it died down. "Have you seen him?"

My chest tightened again for completely different reasons. Thanks to a night with too much champagne, I'd unloaded about Cal. I'd hoped she'd forgotten.

Part of me wanted to lie. To deny I'd seen him plenty, let alone that I'd gotten tangled in his sheets. The other part wanted to dump it all out. So she could confirm that I was a fool and should stay as far away from him as possible.

"I take it by your silence, you have."

"He's friends with my brother." It was true, but felt like a lame excuse.

"And judging by that sour tone, he still makes your heart go pitter-patter."

"I never said that." Pitter-patter was not in my vocabulary.

"Didn't have to."

"You're supposed to let me wallow in denial instead of confronting me." I sank farther down the bed, but I wasn't angry with her. It was why she was such a good friend.

If Lexie knew anything about Cal, she'd have called me out too. Back then, there was something about him being just mine. Like if I talked about our relationship out loud, it would be taken away. I hadn't been willing to risk that, even though I'd needed her so much.

"So-rrry. No denial allowed here," she said unapologetically. "What are you going to do?"

I dropped my chin to my chest and lifted my shoulders in an exaggerated motion as if she could see it.

"Nothing."

And there was the hollow truth. For all my big plans about drop-kicking him after I'd had my fill, it was useless. I couldn't hurt someone who had no feelings toward me.

Wish you'd have realized that before you let him touch you.

I smacked myself in the face. If I wasn't getting payback, I was sleeping with him for me. And if I was sleeping with him for me . . . ugh. Why couldn't I let him go?

"You could forgive him." The suggestion was quiet.

"No."

I didn't want to. The anger I held toward Cal had become a companion. I wouldn't know who I was without it.

"You don't even want to think about it, huh?" she asked, amused.

"Nope."

"I've set you up so many times I've lost count—"

"And I told you before you did that nothing was going to come of it." I appreciated her efforts, all of my friends' efforts, but I wouldn't ever have what some of them did. They were all in committed relationships. Cagan, Bennett, and I were the only single ones. And that was fine by me. Although, none of them, except Cagan, knew about Father's insane plans. Plans that I still had no idea how to get out of.

"You're not the type who needs someone else to be happy, Beau. But as long as you keep holding on to the past, you're always going to be stuck there."

I scowled. "Why do you have to be so reasonable?"

"It's always much easier to solve other people's problems than your own."

There was something in her tone I didn't like. "You know you can talk to me."

"I do, but I can't handle your brutal honesty."

"Yet I'm supposed to take yours?" I asked incredulously.

She laughed, and I did too. "Yes. Yes, you are."

"Of course." I smiled. I had missed her so much.

"So, it's not long until the wedding now. You excited?"

"Super excited. It's been nice seeing my brothers again. And Pepper is so perfect for Teague. He's warmer. Softer somehow. Lincoln too. I like it for both of them."

"I bet. It's your turn next. Do you think they'd come see you in London? It's been years since we saw them."

My turn next. Would they come see me in London? Now that was a question. Would I be "allowed" to return to London was more what Father probably thought I'd be asking. Shit. Two giant albatrosses hanging around my neck.

The doorbell rang in the background. "Oh, shoot. I forgot the plumber was coming this morning."

"I'm glad you called."

"Me too." Her shoes clacked on the hardwood floors. "You're not coming back, are you?"

There was no accusation in her voice. More like she recognized something I wouldn't admit.

"I plan to." Though with every passing day returning to London became more and less appealing. I missed my friends but loved being with my family in New York. Although I might be returning to my life sooner than I thought if I couldn't fix my problem.

"Then we'll be waiting with the welcome mat rolled out."

CHAPTER TWENTY-TWO

CAL

"YO. Anybody actually do any work around here? Maybe I need to put in for a transfer."

Logan Burke sauntered into the station with a cocky grin.

"You can't keep up at this station," Vigiano called as he looked through the cards in his hands.

It was late. Poker chips littered the table. We'd been back from a two-alarm for half an hour and needed to unwind. There'd been a body. Likely dead before the fire, but still.

"I'll run circles around all of you."

"Did you come to stir up shit, Burke?" I flicked my chin. "'Cause I'd say it's a success." I threw a chip at him and grinned when it bounced off.

"I don't do nothing if I can't be the best." He peered at Vigiano's cards, then pointed at them and silently shook his head like it was the worst hand he'd ever seen.

"You're the best at eating." Brennan whacked him in the stomach.

"Just because none of you can cook, don't take it out on me." He smacked Brennan lightly in the back of the head.

"How does Hollingsworth put up with your ass all the time?" I looked through my own cards. My hand was crap too.

Burke turned around and shook his tail. "Nice, ain't it?"

Poker chips, peanuts, napkins, and anything readily available flew in his direction. He laughed and wiggled his ass again for effect.

Crazy SOB. He cracked me up.

"Actually, I came to see you, Cal."

"Whooooo!" All the guys called.

I stood and tossed my cards on the table. "Grow up, boys."

But I didn't want them to. This was our brotherhood. Acting like teenage idiots was one reason I loved them.

I pointed toward the door with my head, which got another round of cat calls.

Burke grinned and flicked them off as he followed me.

"What brings you over to this part of the world?" I led him though the garage, past the fire trucks, and out the back door.

"Just thought I'd see if I'd fall off the edge of the earth if I wandered over here." He smirked and sat in one of the chairs by the back entrance.

"Experiment is a success." I turned a chair around and sat backward. "Go figure."

"Go figure." He looked down, smirk gone. "How's Joe?"

The department was like a small town. My family was well-known, not only because of Pop and my grandfathers, but when there were six of us, it was hard not to be noticed. Joe was a good captain. Respected.

I'd tried to call a few times and gotten no answer. Ma said he'd come by for dinner last night but wouldn't stay. And wouldn't tell her where he was going.

"About as good as anyone in his position." The entire situation was shit. But Joe wouldn't want people, especially anyone in the department, to think he couldn't handle himself.

"Stanis got what was coming to him," Burke said quietly.

A fight like that could divide, especially in our line of work. It wasn't like a normal job. We depended on each other because it was life or death. We were brothers. And when two were fighting, sides were drawn.

But knocking up your best friend's wife? Nobody would side with that.

"Maybe. Didn't fix anything though."

He nodded. "Don't guess much would." He leaned forward, putting his forearms on his knees. "Can't believe they'd do that to Joe. He's one of the good ones."

He was. I'd learned a long time ago that life wasn't fair though.

"He'll be all right." Maybe if I said it enough times, it would be true.

Burke knotted his fingers together, his gaze wary when he looked at me. "You know I've got a friend in the investigation unit."

"The lab lady. Sorry, I forget her name."

There was never quiet in this city. Not even after midnight. But somehow, when there was a little less noise, it seemed hushed. Almost peaceful.

"Willa."

I pointed at him. "That's it."

He cleared his throat. "An investigation like this is hard, especially when it's one of our own."

"Yeah." It was still surreal that Joe's house had burned to the ground on top of everything else. My brother deserved a break. "Any suspects yet?" I had my assumptions—suspicions—but hadn't mentioned them to anyone.

Burke pressed his foot into the ground, then rocked it back to the heel. Heel. Toe. Heel. Toe. "They're . . . uh . . . they're looking at a couple of possibilities, but it's hard when everything is ash."

"Not much to go on. Other than circumstance."

He rubbed his chin. "Somebody said Joe's staying with you."

"He did the night of the fight."

"And the fire," Burke added.

"Yeah. And the fire."

He opened his mouth and closed it a few times. "You sure he was at your place the whole time?"

"I'm sure." I straightened, narrowing my gaze on my friend. "What are you getting at?"

"They—they found something of Joe's at the scene."

"It was his house. I'm sure they found a lot of his things there," I said, voice rising.

"His lighter. At the point of ignition," he blurted as if it was painful.

I shot up from the chair, knocking it over. "Are you accusing my brother of setting fire to his own house?"

Joe would not do that. He wasn't stupid. He knew the risks. Knew how investigations went too.

Burke hung his head. "I'm not." He lifted his eyes. "But I thought you should know he's the primary suspect."

CHAPTER TWENTY-THREE

BEAU

"THESE FLOWER ARRANGEMENTS WOULD BE PERFECT."

Mrs. Davenport fingered a rose in the massive arrangement. If they were in the middle of the tables for the reception, no one would be able to see the person across from them. Maybe that wouldn't be a bad thing.

I made a noncommittal noise.

Father, Alex, and Mr. Davenport were having drinks by the bar, while I was stuck with this woman who had transformed their home into a florist shop. And bakery. And restaurant. There were samples of everything needed for a wedding.

Other than the fact I despised her taste, she may have actually missed her calling.

It didn't matter whether I preferred the arrangement or not. I wasn't marrying Alex. Even if I were, I had no say in any of this.

I suddenly realized how Pepper felt when Miss Adeline and I had thrown a million ideas at her for her wedding. She'd been overwhelmed and miserable. Because it was her day. And while we'd had our hearts in the right place, we'd gone overboard.

I needed to make sure I apologized to her.

Funny how it took being in her position to understand how she felt.

Mrs. Davenport grimaced when my phone chimed with a text. I, on the other hand, was more than happy for an excuse to get away from her. Who would've thought joining my father at the bar with my not-so-future-husband would be more appealing.

Now.

My stomach fluttered. It had been two days since I'd seen or heard from Cal. That one word sent a shot of excitement through me. *Because it's an excuse to get out of here.*

I'd take any reason at this point. Even Cal.

"Excuse me," I said, holding up my phone. "I need to see to this."

I tried to keep my steps neutral as I crossed the room, though it was hard to contain the thrill that one word had sparked.

"Did you find the perfect arrangement, sweetheart?"

The endearment on my father's lips only momentarily soured my mood.

"I think so, Daddy." My smile was only partially fake. In a few minutes, I'd be out of this hellhole.

"Very good. I want you to be happy."

Liar. He wanted *him* to be happy. And that meant this wedding going off without a hitch.

"Thank you." I bent and kissed his cheek. "Something has come up at work. It can't wait."

His nostrils flared in displeasure, though he kept himself controlled. "Nothing is more important than this wedding."

It was a sharp reminder to keep in line.

"Mrs. Davenport has such impeccable taste, she's made it a dream to finalize the details," I said brightly. "I guess when it's the right person, everything falls into place."

Father's hard gaze bore into me, yet he'd managed to keep the rest of his facial features pleasant. "Whatever it is, it can wait until tomorrow. I'm sure you and Alex want to spend time together after dinner."

Is he insinuating I should sleep with that jackass?

I had news for him. This was as close as I'd ever get to that bastard again.

"Darling, I had something special planned."

It was all I could do not to gag when Alex spoke. I wouldn't even think about what that meant and I sure as hell wasn't his darling.

"Let someone else see to the matter. It will be a good test to see who's fit to replace you."

My jaw tightened. My father was going to take away everything I'd worked for. And by the gleam in his cold eyes, he was looking forward to it. Shouldn't he have faith that no one could do my job as well as I did?

"I can't do that."

Disobedience in front of others was strictly forbidden. *Father knows best.* But I had wasted enough time with these people. I had a life to live and I was sick of being so careful to make sure I didn't displease my father.

Be smart about this, Beau. You can get what you want. Just don't rock the boat too much.

I wanted to sink the boat.

Instead, I put on a winning smile. "Would you mind if I borrowed my father for a moment?"

"Of course not, dear," Mr. Davenport said.

Father clutched his drink and led us toward the foyer. "This is unacceptable."

"I didn't want to discuss our business in front of them," I said, keeping my voice low. "It's ours. Not theirs."

That seemed to loosen him up a fraction. And it was actually the truth. The Davenports would never have any say in Hollingsworth Properties.

"What is so urgent?"

"I haven't mentioned it, but I'm working on a development of a new seaport in London. I'm very close to securing the property. Once I do, it will be very lucrative for us." I'd tossed around the idea with Cagan. That counted, right?

He lifted a brow. "What's the issue?"

"I've kept our names a secret from the owner of the property to keep from paying a premium. I don't know if he's become privy to that, but he suddenly wants a lot more money. I don't want to lose this deal."

"Why haven't you mentioned you were pursuing this before now?"

Because I just made it up?

"I didn't want to bother you with it until I was certain things were going to happen."

He scrutinized my face and it felt like my every thought was laid open for him to read. "It's after midnight in London."

"Our business has no set hours."

"If it's lucrative as you say, I want it done."

I nearly sagged in relief. Where was I going to find a property to put a seaport on in London?

I'd worry about that later.

"Yes, Daddy." I kissed his cheek again. This time it didn't feel quite so forced. I was almost free of this sham of an evening. "Give the Davenports my best, please."

He nodded, though his fingers were tight around his drink. "You will make it up to Alex."

When hell freezes over. He was the one who had lots to apologize for to me.

"You're more than welcome to use my father's study if you need." Alex appeared in the doorway, gracious and accommodating.

"I'm afraid this requires my attention at the office." I didn't even care if I sounded apologetic except for my father's benefit. Alex wished he was as intimidating as Samuel Hollingsworth.

"How disappointing." He pushed off the doorframe. "At least let me walk you to your car."

"Not necessary, but thank you," I said quickly. I'd managed to avoid being alone with him all night and intended to keep it that way.

"My car is waiting outside," Father said.

Damn. I'd have to take it.

"I'll escort you." Alex offered his arm.

I ignored him and collected my purse from the entry table before opening the front door.

We were barely outside before he grabbed my elbow. Hard.

"Kindly remove your hand." The words were controlled, but there was no mistaking the fury behind them.

"When we're married, you will not run off to work at every turn." He squeezed, leaning closer. "You will go where I say, when I say."

I glared at him, resisting the urge to back away.

"You will please me. Understood?"

I yanked my arm, but his grip was too tight. His teeth gleamed in the moonlight when he grinned.

"No one comes above my father."

It was a bitter truth. One I hated to admit, even though it was convenient for the moment.

His features darkened. "My wife will do as I say."

"You don't want to upset him."

"You'll make sure he isn't."

Pain shot through my arm as he applied more pressure.

"Who do you think is of more consequence? Me? Or you?" I didn't bother with false pleasantries. There was no need, though I didn't want him to see the rage boiling inside me. "He is a very powerful man."

"And as long as you keep me satisfied, we'll have no issue."

My stomach turned at the insinuation. Was I bound to make the men around me happy? Was that my duty in life?

He mashed his mouth to mine. I turned my head, but he grabbed my chin, and forced me to take the kiss. The pain in my arm shifted to my face and his crushing hold. I beat his chest with my fist, but that only seemed to excite him.

He tasted of stale whiskey as he jabbed his tongue into my mouth over and over.

Stop.

I screamed in my head, but no one could hear it.

The harder I shoved, the harder he held me in place. My jaw felt like it was going to crack.

Get away. Get away. Get away.

He pulled on my hair, and my fists flew more wildly. Another jab into my mouth with his tongue. I bit as hard as I could.

The whiskey taste was replaced with blood.

"You bitch!" He shoved with such force that I stumbled to the ground.

My shoes fell off as I scrambled up. I'd lost my purse, but my phone was still clutched in my hand. I ran with as much speed as I could muster down the front walk. The rocks that stabbed the bottom of my bare feet were nothing compared to the pain in my arm and face.

I glanced back.

Alex was still doubled over. And a figure was in the front window.

My father had witnessed the whole ugly scene and did nothing to stop it.

The shame was worse than any bruise or fractured bone. I'd taken such pride at how strong I was. But when that bastard forced himself on me, I'd stood there and taken it like a weak, pathetic person.

I sprinted toward the park. I couldn't go to Lincoln's. Couldn't let him see that I hadn't been able to take care of myself. My father wouldn't do anything to Alex, but Lincoln would kill him without blinking. Teague would do the same.

I collapsed on a bench. My hand shook as I dialed. I needed help.

"P-p-pick me up at East 83rd and Park."

CHAPTER TWENTY-FOUR

CAL

I SPED through the red light, laying on the horn as I blasted through the intersection.

Two blocks.

Hang on, baby sister. I'm almost there.

My adrenaline pumped through my veins at lightning speed. Beau was the strongest person I knew. I'd never heard her voice quaver. Not even all those years ago.

But that single sentence had scared the life out of me.

I'd driven in record time, couldn't even remember how I'd gotten here.

Her slender form came into view. She was hunched, like she wanted to be invisible. Not the confident woman I knew.

I skidded to a stop, leaned over, and opened the passenger side door. She shook as she climbed inside.

Some of her hair was loose from where she had it pulled back, like it had been yanked free. She had no shoes. No purse.

What the hell happened to you, Beau?

She refused to look at me.

A car turned, the headlights shining on her face. The pink of her lipstick was smeared on her cheek.

I white-knuckled the steering wheel as the pieces added up to a full picture.

Rage like I'd never felt burned every cell of my being.

She closed the door. I crept forward but pulled into the first empty spot on the street.

"Keep driving. As far away from here as you can."

I didn't recognize her voice. Pain was laced in every syllable and it stabbed at the heart I didn't think I had anymore.

"Are you okay?"

It was the dumbest question ever asked. One look at her and I knew she wasn't.

I touched her knee and she flinched. "Tell me what hurts."

What I wanted to know was who did this to her. The demand for answers was on the tip of my tongue. But she was the most important thing right now.

I'd find out who laid a finger on her. And they'd regret the day they ever did.

"D-drive. Please."

Against my better judgment, I did as she asked.

I was trained to handle stressful situations. How to stay calm and keep a level head. I did it every day.

But I could barely keep the truck in my lane. I ran another red light, this time not on purpose, and narrowly missed another car.

Concentrate, asshole. Keep her safe.

Is anything broken?

Who did this?

How badly are you hurt?

Who did this?

Should I take her to the hospital?

Who did this?

I won't let anyone touch you again.

Who did this?

My erratic thoughts matched my wild heartbeat. The silence was awful, but she didn't need me to push. She hadn't called me because she wanted me. I was her last resort, and I wouldn't delude myself into thinking otherwise.

Whether I was first choice or last didn't matter.

She needed me.

I wouldn't let her down again.

Her phone rang. She jumped like she was terrified of everything.

I glanced at the screen.

Father.

She didn't move. It was almost as if she no longer heard the ringtone echoing in the car.

No sooner than the noise stopped, it began again.

She remained still, staring straight ahead.

Had he done this to her?

It rang for a third time, but there was no notification for a voicemail once the noise ceased.

A text message flashed on the screen.

Answer when I call.

She didn't read it.

Say something. Say something that will let her know everything is going to be all right.

The words wouldn't come. She'd always stolen my thoughts, but this was different. I felt helpless.

Once again, I'd driven without remembering how I'd gotten here. My building came into view. I parked in an empty spot a few blocks away.

Shit. She had no shoes.

Did she want to stay in the car?

Once upon a time, she'd felt safe here. But I needed light to see just how much damage was done.

I opened her door and scooped her into my arms. Her phone fell from her hand onto the seat. I shoved it in my pocket and cradled her like she was the most important thing on this earth.

Please don't let any of the neighbors be out.

I didn't need them prying into my business, especially when they'd already had their fill for the week.

I unlocked the door to the building and took the steps two at a time until we reached my floor.

Old Man Casey heaved his trash into the chute. He made a disgruntled noise, but thankfully didn't say anything as he shuffled past.

I shoved in my front door and flipped on the light switch.

Beau blinked.

I nearly lost my sanity.

Blood.

It stained her lips.

And it wasn't one cheek smeared with pink lipstick. Both were.

A faint purple hue dotted her jaw.

Her hair had definitely been pulled.

The hollowness of her dark eyes was the final blow.

None of the fire lit her irises.

He'd taken away her fire.

I would take away his. As soon as I found out who was responsible.

Gently, I placed her on the couch.

I wet a washcloth with warm water and found a bottle of peroxide in the medicine cabinet.

Rage.

I could barely move, I was so blinded by it. If she didn't need me, I'd tear this city to pieces until I got my hands on the son of a bitch who hurt her.

We need photos.

So that asshole couldn't get away with this. And she couldn't pretend it hadn't happened. But I couldn't take them without her consent. And I didn't know how to ask without hurting her. Photographs were personal and invasive.

She lay curled on the sofa where I'd left her. The only indication there was any life inside her was the stilted rise and fall of her chest.

Carefully, I lifted her head and placed it on my lap. With the lightest touch, I wiped the lipstick from her face. She winced, but didn't complain.

"I'm sorry. I'll do this as quickly as I can."

I willed my hand to stay steady, but my anger burned so hot I could barely contain it. At least once I cleaned the blood off her lower lip there was no cut beneath it. I couldn't readily find anywhere the skin was broken.

I hoped she'd gotten a good lick in on whoever did this.

Ever so slowly I pulled the elastic from her hair. She hissed. I took a deep breath to regain control of my emotions.

"Want it back up?" I asked gruffly. She'd hate leaving her hair in disarray because someone had pulled it. I was going to fix it.

She nodded with the slightest of motions. I took extra care not to pull as I piled her hair into a ponytail. It was messy, but another visible reminder of what happened gone.

I took the peroxide and washcloth back to the bathroom and froze.

Had she been raped?

I swallowed around the knot in my throat. Had I just seen that she'd been roughed up because I couldn't think beyond that?

Her clothes were dirty, but not torn. Did that mean anything?

I slammed my fist into the counter. One of the tiles busted, but I barely felt it.

Who had done this to her?

Who touched her with such force that her face was already bruised?

That she lost her purse. Her shoes.

Who the hell did this?

I stalked to my room and grabbed a T-shirt and sweatpants.

Whiskey.

Maybe she'd want a little to calm her nerves. Except she was already calm.

I dropped a few cubes of ice in a glass and covered them with amber liquid.

She was still frozen where I'd left her, staring at nothing.

"Drink a little of this," I said quietly.

She got a whiff of the whiskey and smacked the glass from my hand. My brows shot up as the tumbler hit the carpet. Ice and liquid scattered.

I dropped to my knees in front of her. "I'm sorry. I didn't know."

"I never want to see whiskey again." She spoke in a monotone voice.

I tightened my jaw. "Then you won't." I'd make sure of it. I gripped my thighs, desperate to touch her, but I didn't want to upset her. "Were you—" I struggled to speak the one word. Unprepared for the answer if it was a yes. "Raped?"

She slightly shook her head. I let out a long exhale of relief.

"Can I change your clothes? I brought some sweats. You used to like those."

An image of a younger Beau lounging in my clothes calmed me a little. I'd always liked her in my clothes. Like she was mine.

But the truth was, I'd always been hers.

She sat up and turned so I could reach her zipper. How many times had I done this over the past few weeks? As much as I loved her body, it wasn't about gratification. I needed her to feel cared for. Protected.

As I lowered the zipper, I checked her skin for any marks and was relieved to find none on her exposed back. I pushed her dress down her shoulders and unsnapped her bra.

I was careful as I pulled on the sleeve. *That bruise on her jaw is getting darker.*

"Ahh." She grabbed her elbow.

"I didn't mean to hurt you," I said, panicked at the pain on her face.

A circle of deep purple tainted the skin around the crook of her arm. I balled my fist, ready to commit murder all over again.

"Can you move it?"

"I-I don't know." She stared at her injury.

If it was broken—*Keep it together, Cal. Losing your mind won't help her.*

"Try for me. Just a little."

Gingerly and so damn brave, she bent her arm. Her features

twisted in gut-wrenching pain, but I was pretty sure it wasn't broken. I'd need to get an ice pack on that arm soon though, otherwise she wouldn't be able to lift it in the morning. I hated what I suspected. Her dad had been following her the other night. I knew what domestic violence looked like. Putting two and two together . . .

Did Teague know?

I freed her arms and scanned her exposed torso in a clinical way. No bruises or scratches. Thank God.

I slipped the T-shirt over her head. She only made a tiny noise of discomfort.

When I removed her dress and pulled on the sweatpants, I noticed her filthy feet. I'd been so focused on her face, I forgot to clean her feet.

"Mind walking to the bathroom?"

She took my outstretched hand and leaned on me as I led her down the narrow hall. She limped but was so damn tough. How far had she run without shoes?

A fresh wave of rage that she was in this position threatened to take me under. That someone didn't respect and value Beau for the treasure she was.

I put the stopper in the bathtub with too much force and turned on the hot water. I situated her on the edge of the tub, found another washcloth, and pushed the sweats above her knees.

I tested the temperature. When it was ready, I squirted body wash on the damp cloth and cleaned her feet. There were a few cuts on the bottoms, which I put antiseptic on.

I spread toothpaste on my toothbrush and scrubbed with light circular motion. She closed her eyes as I brushed her teeth like she was in some silent prayer of gratitude.

I pointed to the tub and she spit. I wiped her mouth with a hand towel before taking her back to the living room.

She curled against me, her body small and fragile as I held her.

I kissed the top of her head and willed my thundering pulse to slow down. *Relax. She doesn't need to feel your stress.*

She was safe. She would heal. No one would touch her again. Not on my watch.

"You don't have to tell me right now, baby sister. But I won't let him hurt you again."

He'd never lay a hand on her again.

CHAPTER TWENTY-FIVE

BEAU

EVERYTHING HURT.

Especially my face.

And arm.

And feet.

I kept my eyes closed. A fresh wave of shame washed over me. I'd let Alex Davenport manhandle me like a rag doll. And not only that, I'd run from him like a scared little girl. I should have screamed at him, let his parents see what their precious monster had done to me. And if I didn't grow a backbone, he'd believe he could do it again.

I was so angry.

At him.

At myself for running.

I screwed my eyelids tighter, which pulled on my jaw. Pain bolted from my chin to just below my ear. I stiffened but didn't let out the cry I wanted to.

"What hurts?"

Cal's voice was scratchy from sleep. I froze.

We were tangled together, his body wrapped around me like a protective cocoon.

Please let the entire thing be a nightmare.

It was humiliating enough Alex had overpowered me, but I'd called Cal when I was in trouble? I didn't want to face that either.

His lips brushed my ear. "Are you gonna keep pretending to be asleep?"

Maybe.

It was better than reality.

Sunlight peeked through the curtains. I couldn't stay here, but I didn't want to go. I'd slept, feeling safe shielded by his arms, my fear gone.

Alex couldn't touch me here.

My father couldn't.

And Lincoln and Teague didn't have to worry.

Tenderly, he kissed the side of my head. "I don't have another shift for two days, so I can stay right here until then."

The prospect was tempting.

I wasn't ready to face the world.

Or Cal.

But I had to.

I twisted in his arms, unprepared for the sight of his messy hair, and stubbled jaw, and the intensity staring back at me.

"I'm sorry—"

His expression turned hard. "You don't have a damn thing to be sorry for."

His touch was the opposite of his look. So lightly I barely felt it, he brushed his thumb over my jaw. And I swore the wrath of God was in his eyes.

On one level, I understood his anger. I may not like Cal, but he wouldn't tolerate any woman being harmed.

This was beyond gentlemanly concern.

I felt it.

And it scared me.

"Tell me what happened." He secured his arm around my waist, a protective force that made me feel a safety I wasn't sure existed.

I didn't want to relive last night.

Yet the images flashed through my mind on a repeat reel like it was happening all over again.

Cal kissed my forehead, soothing some of the pain.

I took in a ragged breath and exhaled it shakily. But my chest constricted so tight it was as if someone was standing on it.

"In and out," he said, mimicking the breathing technique he wanted me to follow.

I tried, and after a couple minutes, I was still rattled, but better.

"Thank you for coming when I called." I looked down. There had been so much ugliness between us. "I don't know what I would've done without you."

"I'm glad you did," he said gruffly.

"Teague and Lincoln—"

"Won't do half of what I will to that son of a bitch."

There was murder in his voice. It should've frightened me. But it was my lack of protest that terrified me. Because I wanted Alex to suffer just like he'd made me suffer.

"How bad is it?" I whispered.

I couldn't look to see the damage he'd caused. My arm I could cover up, but my face? I wasn't that creative.

"Makeup won't cover it," Cal said through his teeth.

My face felt tender and swollen. The revelation wasn't a shock but was still a disappointing blow.

I had to think. How was I going to avoid my brothers for a few days? I couldn't go to Lincoln's in this shape.

Though part of me wanted to march into Hollingsworth Properties and force my father to look at what he'd done. Maybe he hadn't laid a finger on me, but he'd put me in this position.

He'd watched. And done nothing.

The hatred I'd felt for Cal seemed dim in comparison to what I felt toward my father. At least Cal had had the decency not to torment me with mind games. It had nearly killed me when he let me go, but he hadn't dragged it out.

Father weaved between little things he'd say and do that made me believe he cared so that when he was awful, it made me doubt myself and my judgment. It was a constant push and pull. A love and hate. And I'd allowed it to continue because he was the only parent I had left. I *wanted* us to have a good relationship. I didn't know how to stop the vicious cycle we were in.

"This wasn't the first time, was it?" The question was lethally quiet.

"It doesn't matter—"

"Are you taking up for him?" Cal roared. "He was a step away from bashing in your face. What's after that? He kills you? Your dad shouldn't—"

"No," I shouted, then clutched my jaw to numb the pain. Had I said that out loud? Because he was right. My dad shouldn't have allowed that maniac to touch me. Surely he'd be calling off the wedding now. Surely he wouldn't entrust me to that . . . asshole. Surely I was worth more to my father than that.

Cal closed his eyes and turned his head as if trying to collect himself. "You haven't seen the damage." When he looked at me again, it took my breath. "You're too precious to be broken."

My nose tingled.

I hadn't shed a single tear through the whole ordeal. Leave it to Cal to say something sweet, to make me feel appreciated, and I was close to the flood gates opening.

I put my forehead to his chest and scooted closer. I needed to forget. To regroup. To think.

And as much as I didn't want to admit it, the only thing that made me feel safe was Cal.

Garrett.

And I felt welcome. *Wanted.*

You're too precious to be broken.

Maybe to Garrett I was.

CHAPTER TWENTY-SIX

CAL

"YOU WANT ME TO ANSWER THAT?"

Her phone lit for no less than the twentieth time this morning. It was barely noon. And most of the calls were from the same person.

Her father.

"No."

Did he often treat her like this?

And if so, how had Teague and Lincoln never seen this? Never done anything?

Do I have this all wrong? Could it be someone other than her father?

I didn't know because I'd given up that right a long time ago.

It wasn't fear in her expression when her father called her. It was anger. Annoyance. Nothing like the terror I saw in her expression last night.

What was going on? She was close to Teague. Surely he would have noticed...

Beau huddled in my sweatshirt on the sofa. She pulled a blanket around her as I rifled through my wallet for money to order Chinese takeout.

She didn't seem to notice the incessant calls. Maybe she was just used to them.

Beau had always been larger than life. Now, she seemed small. Her presence was still a force unlike any other, but there was a vulnerability I'd never seen. I'd had glimpses when she gave herself to me. My touch could soften her like nothing else. But this woman?

I hated the circumstances, but I liked that she needed me. Liked that when she was in trouble, she'd called me. Because when we'd been together, the hard truth was, she *didn't* need me.

I was always the one who needed her.

Not so long ago, I'd been worried about bringing her to my apartment. It was old, but what I could afford. She didn't seem uncomfortable on the hand-me-down sofa.

Last night, I'd acted on instinct. It hadn't occurred to me not to bring her into my space. To be concerned over what she might think. Of how dangerous it would be for me once she was gone.

Because her presence would linger.

But getting her healthy was all that mattered. I'd deal with the fallout later.

"Still Kung Pao shrimp for you?" I held up a menu to the restaurant down the street.

Her brow shot up.

Yeah. I remember everything about you.

She nodded, and I ordered.

Once I joined her on the couch, I discreetly tried to examine her wounds. There were two bruises on her jaw that were darker than the others.

Anger filled me all over again.

"You don't have to pretend you're not checking out my bruises."

I touched a faint purple mark. "I was trying not to remind you they're there."

"Like I could forget," she whispered.

"Hey," I said softly, hating her pain. "You will. I'm not gonna let you remember."

The first sign of that familiar fire flashed in her eyes. "Oh no? Are you planning to stick around?"

I never really went anywhere.

"Are you?"

It wasn't a fair question. This right here was more than we could ever have. She had another life half a world away. Even if she stayed in New York, it might as well be another planet. Her stay in this part of the city was temporary.

She belonged in a penthouse on the park. Not some shithole with a fireman who scraped by.

"You left me."

With words, she was right. I had. But where it counted? I balled my fist. It didn't matter anymore.

"You really think it would've worked out?"

We were sitting so close we touched, but I felt the distance growing between us. And I should be happy it was. I couldn't have her. When she was this close, it was easy to forget that.

She lifted her chin. "I guess we'll never know."

"We know, baby sister. We know." I put a hand on her thigh, careful not to squeeze.

Her dad had followed her, but if it wasn't him who inflicted these wounds . . . who did?

Someone who she was out with when she called me. Someone she ran away from, even leaving her purse behind. She knew him. Clearly. But Beau wasn't a cheater, so surely she wasn't in a relationship with this guy. Besides, Teague would have mentioned someone if she was. "Who is he . . . to you?"

Her eyes flared. "I'm not with some asshole who beats women." Then she covered her mouth with her hand, horror transforming her features. "I didn't fight. I wanted to, but I froze."

Something in my chest cracked. I knew just how hard it was to admit that, not only to me, but to herself.

"You got away." I took her uninjured fingers in mine. "So you must have done something to fight."

I hoped it equated to him never being able to have children.

"I don't think I'm the person I thought I was."

A long time ago, she hadn't been afraid to tell me everything she was thinking. I'd lost that privilege and couldn't believe she was opening up to me now.

"Who do you think you are?"

Her shoulders slumped. "I thought I was strong and smart and . . . brave."

"Keep thinking that." She was every one of those things and more. "But you forgot all fire, independent, and fearless."

"I-I'm not."

I squeezed her fingers. "You are."

"Why didn't I fight him?" She pleaded with me for answers I didn't have.

Her phone lit again.

Lincoln.

"I should answer that. He'll worry."

I picked up the phone and handed it to her.

"Are you at the office? I wanted to run something by you but couldn't find you."

She cleared her throat. "Um, no. I got a lead on some property and went to check it out. What's on your mind?"

"I stumbled on another building in the Bowery. If you're around, I hoped you'd preview it with me."

She fiddled with the blanket. "Send me the specs. If I finish up here soon, maybe we can check it out."

Beau was wrong. She was strong and brave. Hearing her voice, the way she spoke to her brother, no one would ever know the hell she'd been through.

"Call me. And don't forget Eric's piano lesson. He's been talking about it all day."

She screwed up her face in disappointment. "I won't."

She ended the call and tossed the phone beside her. "Can you go to the drugstore? I need some foundation."

"Some what?"

"It's makeup."

"You want me to go buy you makeup?" I asked as if she'd requested I navigate a spaceship to the moon.

Something lightened on her face. "Are you afraid of cosmetics?"

I stared at her incredulously. "Hell yeah, I am."

She laughed. The sound was a rocket back to the past. I'd never taken it for granted, but never thought I'd hear it again.

"But you aren't scared to run into a burning building?"

"Nope."

"The makeup aisle at the drugstore?"

I shuddered. "Terrifying."

She snickered. "I almost want to go with you just to witness it myself."

My brow furrowed. "You'll really love it if I run into one of the guys from the station."

Her eyes widened in mock-horror. "Really, really love it."

If going to the drug store to buy makeup put that smile on her face, I'd do it every single day.

CHAPTER TWENTY-SEVEN

BEAU

"MISS HOLLINGSWORTH. THESE ARE FOR YOU."

The spray of roses and baby's breath nearly took up the entire reception desk. I was actually grateful, hoping they blocked the receptionist's view of me.

Cal had done pretty well with the shade of foundation, but he was right. The bruises had been nearly impossible to cover up.

He'd stayed right with me in the bathroom as I'd faced my injuries for the first time. And I appreciated all the support he'd given me.

His thoughtfulness was almost too much to take. He'd even bought some flip-flops at the drug store because I'd lost my shoes.

He'd been there when I needed someone. I wasn't quite sure what to do with that.

Looking in the mirror at what Alex had done hadn't been easy. It was a reminder of my failure to stand up for myself. But it also renewed my determination.

You forgot all fire, independent, and fearless.

I wouldn't again. Not if I could help it.

I pulled the card from the arrangement. The girls sent me flowers every year on my birthday, but that wasn't today.

I ripped the envelope, curiosity taking over.

Forgive me, love. I'll see you tonight. - Alex

The note fluttered from my hands. Slowly, I backed away from the poisonous arrangement.

Forgive him?

Was he insane? If he thought I was going anywhere near him again, he should be committed.

"Your father wants to see you. He's in his office now."

He was crazy too.

It had taken me over half a day to come to the office. I'd needed to do it. For me. But I wasn't prepared to face Father.

There were so many things I wanted to say. But I couldn't until I decided what I was going to do. I'd worked so hard to build this company. I'd given it so much that it felt like a part of me.

It *was* a part of me.

But last night was an earthquake. The shake I'd needed to wake me up from my zombie state.

I could spout off to Father and lose everything important to me. Or I could take a deep breath and think.

Because I'd had an epiphany when Garrett had been out shopping for me. Something that could actually change the whole trajectory of my life. Our lives.

If Lincoln and I worked together, we could get rid of Samuel Hollingsworth and be free to run this company as we pleased without his iron fist. It might just be possible—

"My office, sweetheart. We have much to discuss."

My stomach knotted. So much for avoidance and deep breaths.

How could he act so controlled, like I was important to him? It only happened in front of other people. And I was so sick of the charade.

"I'm going to view property with Lincoln." I didn't want to be pleasant, but I forced the false cheer into my words and expression.

"This won't take long." He was playing the game too. "Wasn't it thoughtful of Alex to send such a beautiful arrangement?" He flicked his gaze to my feet. "You dropped your card."

I made no move to pick it up. The message had burned me once. I wasn't fool enough to let it happen twice.

"I'll speak to you later." It was a lie. If I had my preference, I'd never talk to my father again.

"I'll come with you. We can share your happy news with your brother."

Bastard.

He knew damn well I didn't want Lincoln or Teague or anyone to know about his master plan to marry me off to Alex Davenport.

Instead of heading toward Lincoln, I caved and moved toward my father's cavernous office. He truly was the king of the city on a magnificent throne.

Father closed the doors and made a production of sitting in his chair. He produced my purse and laid it on his desk.

The object was a glaring reminder of the terror of the night and my failure to fight. I didn't want to touch it, but I picked it up.

"I've spoken to Alex. He understands what he can and cannot do now."

My nostrils flared. The deep breath wouldn't come. Red hot anger surged over as my jaw throbbed.

"What? He can manhandle me as long as there is no physical evidence?" I gripped the back of the chair I stood behind.

A cool stare was all I got in return. Not a single emotion carved his features.

"A quick temper never gets you what you want."

"How about a fractured arm or a bruised face?"

"I've spoken to him about the matter—"

"You've spoken to him," I cried. "You're my father. And you watched him force himself on me." I thrust my finger at him. "You should've defended me. Or at the very least had him put in jail."

Why hadn't I?

I could walk into the station and press charges. My injuries were still fresh.

"Think about how a scandal will harm your brothers."

My mouth dropped open. I shouldn't be surprised by his tactics. They weren't new. But they were effective.

"You mean how it will affect you."

He folded his hands on his desk. "Stay out of the public eye. And you'll be staying with me from this point forward. I'll have Winston collect your things."

I blinked a few times. I didn't know who was crazier. My father or Alex.

"I don't think so. Behind the walls of your house, you might allow Alex to rape me. Did you *speak* to him about those rules?"

His jaw tightened. "That's enough."

"Funny thing. I thought the same thing when he forced his tongue into my mouth. It didn't make a damn bit of difference."

I spun on my heel and strode across the plush rug.

With my hand on the door, I glared back at the man who should've defended me above all others. "When I asked you the first time what you'd do if Alex hurt me, you said you'd hurt him in return. You lied, Father. You watched him hurt me this time, and all you did was *talk* to the asshole."

And that was what was as painful as my physical injuries. He'd told me he'd hurt him, but not only did he do nothing, he failed me. He would always fail me. "In case it wasn't clear, I'm not marrying that son of a bitch."

He sighed as if I were a petulant child. "Your brothers are quite happy, don't you think? More so than I've ever seen."

My blood ran cold.

"I'd hate for that to change. Tragedies are so common now." He sounded like it was such a shame.

He'd allowed a tragedy last night.

Why couldn't you have been killed instead of Mom?

"I will not see him again," I said through my teeth. I loved my brothers. They were my weakness, but they wouldn't stand for this.

Father tapped one thumb on top of the other. "I do wonder if those people were wrongfully put in jail. Maybe your friend did harm that special brother of hers." He picked up his phone. "My conscience won't allow that to stand."

"What are you going to do?"

Evil spread across his face. "The authorities need to know the truth. Abuse against those who are . . ." He pressed his lips together as if searching for the right word. "Vulnerable is such a travesty. Abuse against those poor dogs is too."

He swiped the screen of his phone.

He'd do it. He'd lie and do something awful to Lexie and Pepper. And it would be my fault. They were my friends. I loved them. I loved my brothers.

I could be strong so they could be happy.

Lincoln had done that all of my life for me. It was my turn to let him have the joy he deserved.

"I'm not living with him. And if he ever lays a hand on me—"

"That's the spirit." My father smiled. He'd won. Again. "I'm glad you've come to see things my way."

CHAPTER TWENTY-EIGHT
CAL

"YOU SEEN JOE?"

Bobby slapped my shoulder when I stepped into Ma's living room.

"Uncle Cal. Dad said you're coming to my recital." Nina rushed me, such hope in her gaze.

"Wouldn't miss it."

She threw her arms around me. Teenagers didn't think their old uncles were too cool. It took me a second to catch up, but I hugged her back.

"It's Saturday. Don't forget." She held out her hand. "Give me your phone. I'll set a reminder."

"And it'll go off during the whole damn thing because I don't know how to turn it off."

She giggled, and I pulled on her ponytail.

"Uncle Callll."

My brother nudged me. "She thought you were rad until that comment."

"Rad? Are we back in the nineties?"

He shrugged unapologetically. "Like totally."

"You're such dorks." Nina skipped toward the kitchen.

Had Beau ever been like that? It was hard to picture her so carefree.

My thoughts darkened. *What if some punk roughed up Nina?*

He'd rue the day. Just like the bastard that did it to Beau would... as soon as I found out who he was.

"You look ready to kill someone." Bobby furrowed his brow.

"Long week."

"You're telling me. I had four people out at the station yesterday. Some stomach bug is going around, and my whole crew seems hell-bent on having it." He rubbed the back of his neck. "City won't put in place any kind of rotating measures for when something like this happens. I went into a two-alarm last night myself."

"And you loved being back in the action instead of behind that desk."

He smirked. "Damn straight."

I pinched the flab around his stomach. "You better lay off the sweets if you're going back in."

He punched me in the gut. "I used to have abs like that."

"I don't remember that."

He put me in a headlock. "A wise guy, aren't ya?"

"Boys. Boys. Come set the table."

Bobby got in one more squeeze before we did as Ma said. He pulled my shirt before we crossed the threshold into the kitchen. "You never answered my question," he said in a hushed tone.

"I haven't seen him."

And I should've at least called. But Beau had been my focus. She didn't have anyone else. Joe had my other brothers and Ma to support him when I couldn't pick up the slack.

"I can't get ahold of him."

I frowned. "Did you call the station?"

He rolled his eyes. "Yes, meathead. I called the station. He had the day off. Nobody's talked to him."

"Maybe he just needs a minute alone." A lot had happened. Our family could be smothering. But Joe wasn't a loner type.

Bam. Screeech.

The front door flew open and slammed into the wall.

"Ma! Where are ya? You got anything to eat?" Joe's words were slurred as he stumbled into the living room.

He tripped over the carpet and fell face first, narrowly missing the coffee table.

"Oww." He rubbed his forehead then rolled over on his back.

"Joseph Anthony Calhoun. What in the world is going on?" Ma marched out of the kitchen, hands on her hips.

Nina and Grace were right behind her, peering around to see what the commotion was about.

"Girls, go in the kitchen. Eat your supper before it gets cold," Bobby said.

"What's the matter with Uncle Joe?" Nina asked.

"In the kitchen." Ma herded them to the table.

I took two steps toward Joe and got a whiff of whiskey. He smelled like he'd bathed in the stuff. The stale odor of cigarettes layered on top of it had me turning my head.

"Damn, Joe. Where you been?"

Bobby recoiled. "He's gonna throw up. He always throws up." He took off toward the kitchen.

I squatted and patted Joe's cheek a couple times. He'd passed out.

I hope you didn't drive here.

A loud snore sent another wave of the whiskey cigarette cocktail scent in my face.

"Joe." I patted him a little harder. "Wake up."

Bobby returned with a trash can. "He's still got on his uniform."

"It's not like he has any other clothes," I pointed out. They were all burned except for what I'd packed in his duffel.

"If he's been at Donnovan's, I'm gonna have a word with Roy for not calling one of us. He shouldn't have let Joe get in this shape." Bobby bent forward and grabbed Joe's shoulder. "Let's get him on the couch. I'm not lugging his ass upstairs."

"Ma will kill us if he gets sick on her sofa."

He looked between Joe and the piece of furniture, then shrugged and let our brother fall back to the carpet.

I tried a few more times to wake him up. He swatted at me as he snored.

I looked out the front window. "Shit."

Bobby pulled the curtain back. "Oh, hell."

Joe's car was in the front yard, still running with the lights on. Ma's rose bushes were toast.

"I'll move it around back."

She was going to kill him for driving that wasted.

I jogged down the front steps as blue lights flashed.

Please let them keep going.

The police cruiser stopped in the street next to my Suburban.

How did he manage to get though the parked—oh.

Bobby was going to flip. Joe had smashed the front end of his car so hard it was on the sidewalk. The bumper of Ma's car was hanging off. There was a dent in the trunk so deep I wasn't sure we'd be able to get it open.

Egan and McCreedie rounded their car and sauntered over.

"I'm moving it, fellas." I rested my hand on the doorframe.

"Can't let you do that, Cal." Egan pulled out his flashlight. "He ran two people off the road eight blocks back and scraped a half a dozen other cars before he got here."

"Anybody hurt?"

"A woman and her kid had to go to the hospital. Think they're going to be okay, but we can't let Joe off on one." There was a sorry behind his words, and I appreciated it.

Joe had put them in an awkward position because of their friendship, but he'd crossed a line and this couldn't be swept under the rug.

"I understand."

"Egan. McCreedie. What you doing here?" Bobby joined us on the front lawn.

"Collecting evidence. And we gotta haul Joe in."

"Shit." Bobby put his hands on his hips and turned toward the house. "He's out cold."

"Then we won't even have to cuff him. We'll put him in his own cell."

"Do you have to? It's just his car and Ma's lawn—" Bobby noticed his ride was all kinds of messed up. "I wanna strangle that idiot, but I can't. He's been through enough."

"Sent a woman and kid to the hospital," I said quietly.

He cursed again. "Can we at least get this mess out of here? Half the neighborhood already has pictures. Ma doesn't need this."

"We'll wrap it up as soon as we can. Crime scene unit will be here soon."

Great.

That was just what we needed. A street full of cops at Ma's.

McCreedie pulled me aside. "I get it. I really do. But you gotta get your brother under control before he does something we can't help him out of."

His lighter. At the point of ignition.

Had he already?

CHAPTER TWENTY-NINE

BEAU

"YOU HAVE something purple on your chin."

Eric pointed, peering at my face.

I hadn't been this close to anyone—except Cal—and so far it had worked well. Or people had kept their mouths shut.

I forgot to reapply makeup before the piano lesson with Eric. We sat on the bench together. At that angle, it was probably impossible not to see.

"You work on this and I'm going to try to get it off," I said brightly.

"Okay."

His fingers flew over the keys. He'd taken to the piano as if he was born to play. Eric was gifted beyond measure.

I rushed to my bathroom and examined the bruise. Indeed, it was starting to peek out beneath the makeup. I reapplied, taking extra care to cover up any other bare spots.

Once I was satisfied, I rejoined Eric in the living room. The piece was melancholy and beautiful. It fit my mood as he flawlessly played.

Lincoln and Lexie wandered beside me.

"I thought you were having a date hour," I whispered.

"We are, but the music is too magnificent to ignore," Lexie whispered back. She elbowed Lincoln. "Magnificent is his word."

And he was right.

The doorbell rang. Muffy and Millie raced toward it, barking their heads off.

The music stopped.

"Who's coming over?" Eric asked.

"Are you expecting anyone?" Lincoln looked between Lexie and me.

We both shook our heads.

He strode to the door and checked the spy hole. Then he snapped and both dogs sat, though they continued barking.

"Winston. What are you doing here?" Lincoln ushered the man who'd been more of a father to us than our own had inside. "Forgive me for being abrupt. I'm pleasantly surprised."

Dread filled me. I'd forced myself to shove the conversation with my father into the deepest recesses of my mind. The sight of Winston brought it crashing back with a vengeance.

"I'm here to collect Miss Hollingsworth."

Lincoln furrowed his brow. "I thought you weren't expecting anyone?"

"I forgot. Winston, I'm not ready yet." I touched Eric's shoulder. "Another lesson next week?"

"Okay. Thank you for teaching me."

"You've made the piano not so bad," I said, a little too honestly. I still despised the sight of one but didn't want to ruin it for Eric.

"Where are you going?" he asked.

"To spend time with my father."

"I forbid it," Lincoln growled.

Eric's eyes widened, as did mine.

"I'm afraid you don't have a say in it." I kissed Winston's cheek. "Give me a few minutes to gather my things."

Lincoln's hard footsteps were right behind me. "What is he threatening you with?"

I pulled my suitcase from the closet and stuffed my clothes inside without folding them. "I need to do this."

He spun me, so I was forced to look at him. "No, you don't." Fear was in every line of my brother's expression.

"You need time with Lexie and Eric without me invading your space," I said lightly.

"You're hardly ever here. And this is your home."

I clutched his arms. It was my home. Because my brothers were here.

"I love you. You're the best oldest brother in the world."

"*Beau.*"

"Trust me. Please." I didn't want to leave. Lincoln was protective. Our father was a warden.

"I've learned the difficult way that not communicating is the wrong approach."

My heart twisted. That was Lincoln's way of apologizing for not always being open with me. Unfortunately, I'd learned why he didn't always talk to me about things.

Because there was nothing either of us wouldn't do to protect the people we loved.

"Help me with my suitcase?"

He scowled. "That makes me feel as if I condone this."

"I'm well aware you don't, but I need your support."

"Does Teague know?"

I grabbed my toiletry bag from the bathroom. "He'd have a much worse reaction than you."

Lincoln had learned how to tolerate our father. Teague didn't care to try. Rightly so.

"Are we running you off?" Lexie worried her lip as she leaned in the doorway.

"No. I've promised everyone some time while I'm here. Teague and Pepper's is up next after Father's." *Fake it till you make it, sister.*

If I could make them believe I was voluntarily staying with my father, I deserved an award. Getting to the wedding was going to be interesting. I doubted that Lincoln had mentioned the quick date to Father. "Besides, I can't stay here only days before the wedding. You need me out of your hair so you can focus on all the wonderful things."

"Don't be silly, Beau. We want you here—"

"Lex, one Hollingsworth is enough." She laughed. I couldn't, but I managed a smile. I hugged Lincoln and then Lexie. "Don't give my room away."

"Never." Lincoln clutched the handle of my suitcase. "If he does anything—"

"You'll be the first to know."

Hold it together. Hold. It. Together.

The entire charade was another reminder that for all my bravado, my life was not my own. My father should've been my advocate. He should've buried Alex for what he did. But he hadn't. He'd let me down again.

And it still hurt as if it was the first time he'd done it.

My father didn't care if I stayed with him . . . other than he could watch me more carefully. And somehow he knew I enjoyed the place I had with my brother. In his eyes, that couldn't stand.

Control. Heartless control.

He was taking me away from my brother and my best friend. Like I was a prisoner and happiness was my crime.

I swallowed past the lump in my throat. The motion sent a twinge through my jaw. *You're not brave. If you were, you'd stand up to him.*

And then he'd do something to my family. My *real* family.

I still had time to figure out a way to keep from marrying Alex. But the window was growing smaller.

Maybe the answer wasn't for me to find a solution.

Maybe I needed to get rid of the problem.

CHAPTER THIRTY
CAL

"I'D HIT you upside the head, but my guess is yours already hurts like mad."

Joe groaned when I shook him.

"I'm busting you out. Let's get a move on."

Egan and McCreedie had released Joe from custody after he'd slept off some of the alcohol and given me "friends and family" privilege to get Joe out of his cell at the station.

It was almost dawn. At least one of us had slept.

We'd had an emergency meeting of brothers. Getting Ma to calm down had taken up a lot of our efforts.

When Egan called for me to come pick Joe up, all five of us loaded up in my truck. Didn't matter some of my brothers had shifts that started in a couple hours. We were in crisis.

And the Calhouns stood together.

"Leave me alone, Cal," Joe groaned.

I shook him again. "Can't do that."

He tried to roll over on the tiny mattress, but there wasn't room.

"You gonna make me carry you out of here like a baby?" I shrugged. "Fine. Have it your way."

I slid my arms under him.

"Stop it." He flailed about. "I'll get up."

I stepped back to give him the space to sit up. When he did, he grabbed his head. But after a second, he collected himself and stood.

Without a word, we followed Egan out of the back. He gave Joe a bag of his things, and we moved to the lobby where our brothers were waiting.

"You asshole."

"What were you thinking?"

"Ma's gonna kill you."

"You look like crap."

The reception wasn't sugarcoated, but every word was spoken with back slaps and hugs. We didn't know anything other than tough love.

I hung back as they steered him out of the station toward the car.

I'd texted Beau hours ago.

After a glance at my phone, I saw the same response I'd had before. None.

You should've called her.

When was I going to do that? After I cleaned up the vomit at Ma's or before I picked up Joe from jail?

What if she was with the jackass who'd hurt her? What if she needed me?

I had to trust she wouldn't allow herself to be alone with him again. Except I didn't know anything about what had really happened. All I had to go on was what I saw and the very little she'd told me.

It had taken all I had to let her leave my apartment earlier. But I wasn't her captor and refused to treat her as such. I just hadn't been able to breathe easy since she'd been out of my sight.

Are you in pain, baby sister?

Mike fell in step beside me. "Want me to drive? I snuck in a nap while everybody was arguing about where Joe is going to stay."

"I'm good." I shoved my phone back in my pocket and dug out my keys. "If you need to head home—"

"I already called the station and switched shifts."

I nodded, thankful I had the day off. "Do you think it's a good idea to take him to Ma's?"

She'd insisted and won out over all of us. I didn't want her to be stressed, but there was no doubt she'd keep a watchful eye on Joe. Maybe he needed to go home.

"It's best. I'll stay with them tonight. We can rotate depending on who's working so it won't be so hard on her," Mike said.

We'd do whatever we had to do to help our brother heal.

He pulled on my arm while they loaded Joe in the truck. "I talked to Roy. Christina came into Donnovan's raising all kinds of hell. Then she served him with divorce papers. In front of everybody."

I winced and looked away. No wonder he tried to drown himself in whiskey. The woman had no mercy.

"Wish he'd have called one of us when that happened." If he had, maybe we could've avoided the whole situation.

"Said he tried all of us and couldn't get an answer."

I hadn't had any missed calls. At least I didn't think I had.

"Why did he let Joe leave in that shape?" It was unconscionable. Roy Donnovan was a friend. He and Joe had gone to school together.

"He went to get something out of the back. Thought Joe wouldn't move since he hadn't for a few hours. He came back. Joe was gone."

I plowed a hand through my hair. "Somebody needs to keep an eye on him all the time."

"We'll see him through this."

I just hoped my brother was right.

CHAPTER THIRTY-ONE

BEAU

"CHEERS TO THE BRIDE AND GROOM."

I lifted my champagne flute, tendrils of real joy filtering through me for the first time in I couldn't recall how long.

Lincoln and Lexie were married. They'd pulled it together fast. And I hadn't even been able to live with them to be around to help.

No. I wouldn't think about that.

Happiness. That was the word for the day.

And there was so much of it in this room, it was palpable.

Glasses filled the air, along with cheers of agreement.

I looked around the table.

Family.

Lincoln, Teague, Lexie, Eric, Pepper, and Miss Adeline.

They were my family, and I was so lucky to have them.

"I assume my invitation got lost in the mail."

And just like that, all of the air was sucked from my lungs. He shouldn't be here. He shouldn't try to destroy the beauty of the occasion.

Teague dropped his fork and appeared ready to bodily escort our father out. "You weren't invited."

My brother was the picture of strength. I was in complete awe of his bravery. I'd never be able to say something like that. Not to that monster.

"This isn't an appropriate time." Lincoln's voice was low and serious in a way I'd never heard him address our father.

I was proud of him too. Why couldn't I find my voice to tell Father to get the hell out?

Father rounded the table and picked up Teague's champagne flute. "Surely, you don't expect me to be absent on such a momentous occasion in my children's lives?"

Teague shot from his chair so quickly it scraped against the hardwood floor.

Only moments ago there were happy faces around the table. Now there were hard, angry expressions.

He'd ruined Lincoln and Lexie's wedding.

And it had happened in the blink of an eye.

"Sit down, son. I'm only here for well wishes." Father's evil grin shifted to me. "And to think we get to do this all over again in two weeks. At Beau's wedding."

Ice ran through my veins.

All eyes turned to me, though my focus was on the man who seemed determined to make me miserable. Had he sensed I wasn't going to go through with it? Was this a reminder to fall in line and obey?

"I take it by the silence, I'm not invited to share a piece of cake." Father set down the glass. "We'll do that soon enough."

"You're getting married?" Teague asked carefully.

I looked at him, at a loss. "Excuse me."

I hadn't learned any courage from him at all. Fear. That was all I knew.

That and anger.

I raced to Lincoln's study. It was Eric's room now, and maybe I didn't have the right to enter without permission, but I loved the space too. It was warm and somehow made me feel safe.

"Why is our father showing up to my wedding to announce

yours?" Lincoln marched in behind me. Hurt and concern were etched into his features.

I hadn't wanted him to find out this way. Actually, I hadn't wanted him to find out at all.

I sank down in the chair behind his desk, too exhausted to stand.

He came around and leaned on the edge of the massive wooden piece of furniture. "In two weeks? Is this where you've been going at all hours of the night? Sneaking around with . . . who are you marrying?"

There was one bonus to that announcement. At least it threw him off the trail of who I'd really been spending time with.

Though I didn't care if he knew about Cal. Only that it was temporary so there was no point in dragging my brother into something that was over before it began. Over a long, long time ago.

That familiar ache throbbed in my chest.

What would I say to Lincoln? *You know, Cal. Well, I forgot to mention that way back when he tore my heart to shreds and I'm still humiliated over it.*

"Beau." He spoke with such worry it jolted me from my thoughts.

"It's not a big deal." I shrugged and pretended to study the papers in front of me on his desk.

I didn't have to look up. I *felt* Lincoln's imploring gaze.

"A wedding is quite the *big deal*," he mocked. "Especially when other people know about it before your own brother."

I wanted to tell him everything. That Father was forcing me and I hadn't come up with a way to stop it yet. But I couldn't put that on him.

Teague burst into the office. "What the hell is this?"

I wanted to spin the chair toward the city and pretend they weren't there. Just like Lincoln had done to me once. That had made me furious, but now I understood why he'd done it.

He didn't want to hurt me.

"That's what I'm trying to find out," Lincoln said. "Why wouldn't you tell us?" His tone softened, like I'd wounded him.

I hated that my father had done this. That I'd allowed him to taint my relationship with my brothers.

"It's a recent thing." I waved off as if it were nothing instead of my entire future ruined.

If I married Alex Davenport, I'd likely suffer the same fate as my mother. Only I'd be dead by his hands.

How would Father cover up that?

I slapped my hands on the desk. Pain shot through my arms, but I barely felt it.

Lincoln and Teague started at my outburst.

"Did he cover up her murder?" I whispered.

Lincoln recoiled. "Why would you think that?"

I didn't have to explain what I was talking about. He *knew*.

Teague stumbled back.

"There's no information—"

"This is a discussion for elsewhere," he said sharply.

I narrowed my gaze. "What do you know?"

Was this just something else my big brother kept from me in the name of protection?

He sank into a chair across from my desk. "Not now."

"Did he have her—"

"I don't know. But not. Now." He leaned forward, discussion closed.

We weren't in a safe space to openly talk about it. Father was likely still just down the hall. But Lincoln would never bring up the topic again, no matter where we were.

"Later never comes with you," I muttered. Maybe this hadn't been a good time to bring up her murder. Not on his wedding day, but I was out of sorts like I'd been tumbled about and didn't know which way was up.

"I'm not the only one who isn't forthcoming." He folded his arms and lifted a brow.

"Father introduced me to Alex. We hit it off. The alliance makes sense." *Why don't you tell them the truth?*

I couldn't.

Your brothers are quite happy, don't you think? More so than I've ever seen. I'd hate for that to change. Tragedies are so common now.

My own happiness meant nothing compared to his and Teague's.

"Is this why you came back to New York?" Teague asked, his hurt equaled to Lincoln's.

Unwittingly, yes it was.

"Looks like I'll be moving back to the city. That's a plus, right?" I forced a lightness in my tone I didn't feel.

"It is," Lincoln said through his teeth.

"Don't sound so excited."

He scowled at my sarcasm. "It seems we have a major communication problem."

The only person I didn't have one with was Father. And Cal. I couldn't seem to stop my thoughts from tumbling out around him whether I liked it or not.

"We're working on it." I picked up a file. "I have a bit of good news."

"Besides your pending nuptials?"

I glared. "I've found apartments to relocate the tenants for our Ludlow project. They're nearby and should be suitable. It's a semi-wedding gift. I just hadn't had a chance to tell you yet."

This was not the time to bring this up, but I had to divert attention. I hated what Father had done to Lincoln and Lexie's day. Hopefully this was some good news to get us back to celebrating.

"You found an entire building to house them in?"

"I'm not a miracle worker." I made a *what are you thinking* face. "I searched for several buildings nearby and am in talks with the landlords to finalize the terms." I pushed at the folder on the desk. "I also sent letters to the tenants and plan to go door-to-door to make sure the pertinent information is conveyed."

"When do you plan to do that? I'll go with you."

I rubbed my face. "I'm not sure yet, but I'll let you know."

He craned his neck. "How did you get that bruise on your jaw?"

Dang it. Dang it. Dang it.

"I dropped something and banged it on the desk when I bent to pick it up," I said lightly.

He lifted a brow.

Teague stomped forward, examining for himself. Judging from the flare of his nostrils, he wasn't happy.

I waved a hand in front of my face. "Just a little bump."

It was as if Alex's hands were on me again, tightening their grip. I shuddered as a streak of fear raced through me. I had fourteen days—nearly thirteen now—to avoid marrying him.

What are you going to do?

"I recall someone getting very angry when someone else wasn't forthcoming." Lincoln drilled his gaze into me. "I've made mistakes, and I'm sorry for that. But you can trust me, Beau." He placed a hand on my shoulder. "You don't need me to handle anything, but don't forget I'm here to support you. Teague too."

He waited for an acknowledgement, but all I could offer was a silent nod.

You can't help me with this. If you do, it will hurt the people we love.

"Isn't the guy supposed to ask us permission?" Teague folded his arms.

"He did."

We all turned around.

Father stood in the doorway as smug as I'd ever seen him. "I've given the happy couple my blessing."

His definition of happy and mine were vastly different. *How could a father* bless *the marriage of his only daughter to a man who nearly fractured her jaw and arm?*

Teague looked at me, hurt and stunned surprise on his face. "I didn't even know you were dating anyone."

He spoke quietly. I couldn't bear that I'd hurt him. And he'd all but admitted it in front of our father. That wasn't easy on him.

I didn't want to lie to him. To either of them.

As if Father was in my head, he fired a warning look in my direction. A reminder of what would happen if I strayed.

I cleared my throat. "It's all happened suddenly." Did I sound bright? I hoped so.

Teague narrowed his gaze in a look that rivaled one of Lincoln's. Then he turned it on our father. "You're behind this." Then he pointed at me. "You don't have to do anything he demands."

Oh, but I do. Or you could lose Pepper.

Teague was by far the best at dodging our father's wishes, but even he'd caved for a time.

I'd do anything for my brothers . . . even—I couldn't finish that thought. Time and distance hadn't deterred our bond. They still knew when I wasn't really telling the truth. Knew when I wasn't holding it together, no matter how I tried.

"I'm only looking out for my daughter as any father would."

Don't throw this letter opener at him. Don't throw this letter opener at him.

I schooled my features into a neutral expression as anger simmered beneath my surface.

To think there'd been a time I wanted that man's affection. His attention. A normal relationship where we could talk about . . . whatever fathers and daughters discussed.

And deep down, that longing hadn't gone away.

Until he'd killed it. Standing in a window. Watching a man maul me against my will.

A monster he was still willing to give me away to.

"That's terrifying," Teague said.

Father wrinkled his nose as if he'd smelled something foul.

Teague focused on me. "What's the rush? If this is your guy, bring him over for dinner. Let us get to know him." He motioned toward me. "We already know he's not good enough for you."

I swallowed hard. My eyes stung as I prayed the threatening tears would stay contained.

It was an odd moment for a revelation, but I realized I didn't need all the things I thought I wanted from my father.

Because I was already loved beyond measure by my incredible brothers.

Which was why I had to put them first.

"It's all happening so fast," I whispered. That much was the truth.

"When you know, you know," Father said. We all stared at him. He wasn't one for romantic notions. "Your mother would want you to make the leap and follow your heart."

Not with Alex Davenport. I gripped the armrest of my chair. At least I didn't think she would. I didn't know her. Because no one would tell me anything about her.

I wish . . . what was the point? I'd never have the chance to know her. But the version of her I'd created in my head was nothing like Father.

Although it actually aligned with what he'd said. She would genuinely want me to leap and follow my heart.

"Since you're both so keen to meet your sister's soon-to-be husband, dinner will be arranged." His gaze was like ice when it landed on me. "We'd better do it soon. There isn't much time before the big day."

He disappeared as if he'd vaporized like a demon.

Teague propped a hip on the desk. The concern on his face nearly undid me. "Do you really want to marry that guy?"

The quiet question had the impact of a bomb blast. I didn't make a habit of lying to my brothers. Maybe I didn't tell them things sometimes . . . like about Cal, but I never wanted to intentionally mislead them.

Even Lincoln's normally stone-like features held such worry that all of this mess was on the tip of my tongue.

"A family dinner sounds fun," I said brightly. "Think there's any chance we can uninvite . . ." I waved in the general direction Father slithered away in, unable to speak his name.

Teague shifted toward Lincoln. "What do you know about him? Because I don't believe Beau has suddenly *fallen in love.*"

"I'm about to find out." My oldest brother was terrifying when he wanted to be.

"Both of you suddenly fell in love. Not so long ago, if I'd asked you about getting married, you'd have both grumbled and sworn it wasn't happening," I said, voice rising. What they didn't know was that I was vehemently more anti-relationship than both of them combined. But I'd been burned. I knew what the pain of heartbreak felt like.

Who in their right mind would risk that twice?

Lincoln scowled. "Don't let him force you into something you don't want to do."

Wasn't that what our lives were? A giant game of *Please Samuel Hollingsworth*.

All of our phones chimed at the same time.

Tomorrow evening. 7 pm. Our family home.

There was no way my brothers wouldn't see through the lies tomorrow night. They knew—loved—me far too well. *Damn.*

I reached for Lincoln's hand. "I'm sorry I ruined your wedding."

Gently he squeezed. "You give him too much power. He wishes he could ruin the day for Lexie and me."

I stood and hugged him. "You deserve Lexie and Eric and a lifetime of happiness." I kissed his cheek, then reached for Teague's hand. "You're right. We won't let him ruin that."

Because I'm going to make sure of it for both of you. *He won't steal your happiness, big brothers. Even if it costs me mine.*

CHAPTER THIRTY-TWO

BEAU

"THERE SHE IS."

Father stood from the head of the dining table with a smile so kind it was almost believable.

I'd been summoned. And now it was apparent it wasn't for a father-daughter breakfast.

The Davenports sat near my father, looking pleased to be in the Hollingsworth family home. Not many people made it behind these doors.

Father lifted a brow at Alex, who awkwardly stood too. He came toward me like a predator who knew he had his prey exactly where he wanted them.

Why would my father give him this advantage? We were the ones with the most power. Yet he was handing it to Alex on a silver platter.

"Don't come any closer," I said through my fake smile.

His steps faltered, but he didn't stop. "Did you get my flowers?"

"Did you get my medical bills?" I asked far too sweetly.

His jaw clenched. "It was a little misunderstanding, darling. I'm sure you'll do your best to please me from now on."

What?

I shouldn't have covered up the bruises. I should've made him look at what he'd done.

"Now that you've accepted my generous apology, let's have breakfast." He put a hand on the small of my back and steered me toward my father.

In this massive room, I was trapped. The table and the wall kept me from being able to get away from Alex's touch. Though it was slight, it felt like a steel weight on my back.

Alex presented me to Father like I was some sort of prized pony.

"Good morning, sweetheart." He kissed my cheek. Through the pleasant look was a warning to fall in line.

"Good morning."

I didn't acknowledge the Davenports as I sat across the mammoth table from them. The room was ridiculous. An "intimate" breakfast with future in-laws shouldn't be held at a table for twenty. I almost needed binoculars to see the opposite end.

I should move down there.

"We're so thrilled you want to move the wedding date sooner. That will make the arrangements a bit of a hassle, but we're so close to finalizing details that it should be fine."

I dropped the water glass in my hand.

Sooner? I glanced at Father who had a triumphant gleam in his dark eyes.

Winston rushed over to sweep the glass and mop the water from the floor. I barely felt the liquid that had splashed on my dress.

If anything, my father should have called this entire sham off. Not expedited the wedding.

No. No. No.

"I nearly had the same reaction when Samuel told me," Mrs. Davenport said gleefully. "The invitations went out this morning. We're having them hand delivered so the guests appreciate what an exclusive event this is."

A wave of nausea rolled through me. No. I needed more time.

This-this couldn't be happening.

"We only have a few days to find an apartment, but your father has graciously offered to let us stay here until we find the perfect place." Alex beamed. "What a wonderful wedding gift, sir. We're thrilled."

Why were all the Davenports so thrilled? They were practically salivating.

"Excuse me." I pushed out of my seat. "I need to dry my dress."

"Of course." Father stood and walked me to the foyer. "Collect yourself."

"You moved the date?" I hissed.

"Time is of the essence."

"For what?" I cried.

He scowled in silent warning to keep my voice down. "I want Davenport's company. And you're going to get it for me."

CHAPTER THIRTY-THREE

BEAU

FIVE DAYS.

Five. Days.

The invitations were being hand delivered at this very moment. Meanwhile it was all I could do to settle my racing heart. This couldn't be healthy. I hadn't taken a full breath since . . . actually since I'd left Cal's.

Cal.

I'd ignored his texts checking on me, even though he deserved an answer. I hadn't reconciled the man who'd been so callous in the past to the one who cared for me like I was the most precious thing in the universe.

I pushed out of the coffee shop. Even lavender tea hadn't calmed my nerves. I'd been wandering aimlessly around the city for two hours.

Drive.

As much as I hated it, I needed to take a drive. Not in Lincoln's car. Or in a taxi.

I pulled out my phone and dialed.

"She's alive. I was beginning to wonder."

Underneath that jest, I heard his concern. And the second I heard his voice, the panicked state I'd been in all morning subsided.

"Are you working?"

"I'm off."

I sucked in a deep breath and released it. "Want to go for a drive?"

You are playing with fire, sister.

"Where are you?" Keys jangled on the other end of the line.

I looked at the street signs on the corner. "5th and East 59th."

"Might take me a minute to get there."

I wanted him now. My patience with everything was officially at zero.

"That's fine."

I hung up and wandered over to a nearby bus stop bench.

I should've called Lincoln. He'd know what to do. How to handle Father.

But I didn't want my brother.

I wanted to get lost with Cal so that maybe I could find my way.

What would've happened if he'd never broken my heart? Was he right? Would it eventually have happened anyway?

I tried to picture my life from a different path, one where Cal and I had made it work. The image wouldn't come. The only thing I saw was my twenty-five-year-old self, miserable and hurt.

"I'VE FOUND THE PERFECT APARTMENT."

I rushed toward Garrett and threw my arms around him.

"Are you any good at remodeling? It needs a lot of work, but we can live there while we make it what we want." I'd known the second I set foot inside that it was the one.

"It's almost halfway between the fire station and the office, so neither of us will have to sacrifice on commute time." I was babbling. I knew it. But I was so excited. We could start our life together. Or keep it going.

"You think your daddy is going to let you shack up with a fireman from the Bronx?"

I jolted at the question. A chill went through me. And I realized it was because I was holding on to Garrett, but he wasn't touching me.

"I'll figure it out." *I hadn't thought about telling Father or my brothers in all my excitement.*

A nervous pit formed in my stomach, but at some point, I had to make the leap. Lincoln and Teague would eventually understand once they saw how much Garrett meant to me. How good he was to me.

My father . . . he was a different beast. But it was my life. He'd have to understand too.

"It's been three years. If you were going to tell them, it would've already happened."

I wanted to. But then Garrett became mine. And I was afraid if I shared him, he'd be taken away. Maybe that was selfish and stupid, but we'd had all these good years together. I wouldn't trade them for anything.

"It's not like you've introduced me to your family either. Except your dad." *I threw my hands up. I wasn't the only one who'd kept us a secret.*

"Why would I when this is a dead end?" *He was cold and detached.*

A far cry from his normal warmth.

I took a step back. "A dead end?" *I understood the words but couldn't process them.*

He flashed a cocky smirk. One that made my stomach turn.

"Come on, baby sister. You didn't really think this was more than a little fun?"

Yes. Yes, I did.

It was a lot more than a little fun *for me. I'd given him my heart. And how had the affectionate nickname turned so cold?*

"You don't mean that." *I took another step backward.*

He shrugged. "Might as well end it now. I got what I wanted."

I recoiled as if he'd slapped me. What he wanted?

"And what exactly was that?" *I wanted to shake him. Make him stop. Bring back the Garrett I loved. Because this wasn't him. This was* Cal.

He gave me an unimpressed look. "Want me to spell it out?"

No.

He'd been so careful. Protective. He'd always made me feel safe. And loved.

Never once had he pushed for more than I was ready for. He'd respected my needs above his own.

It was why I'd trusted him with my body.

Now it belonged to him.

So did my heart.

And he was ripping it to shreds.

"Why are you doing this?" I whispered.

We were right together. He filled a piece of me I hadn't known I was missing.

"One day you'll thank me."

The hollowness of the words carried a weight that nearly crippled me.

"Stop."

He let out a long, annoyed sigh. "Don't get stubborn on me. I know you have to have things your way, but this time you don't get to choose."

I never got to choose.

Not what I did, how I dressed, who I loved.

It was all done for me.

Garrett hadn't given me a choice when it came to him. I'd fallen hard and fast before I could even think about it.

Just like everything else, I had no say when it was done.

Because Garrett wasn't a dead end for me. He was the beginning.

"Did my brother say something to you?"

He rolled his eyes. "No, Teague didn't say anything. And don't worry. I'll keep our little secret safe."

His voice was a knife, cutting tiny slices over my whole heart. I was bleeding out and there was nothing I could do.

The pain was too much to stand and my anger took over to mask it.

"I hate you for this." I spoke low and feral. "Don't bother crawling back when you realize what you just threw away."

HE HADN'T CRAWLED BACK. Stupid me had thought he would. Prayed he would. How could he stand the misery?

Except he didn't feel what I had.

I'd been in the relationship alone when I thought we were partners. He'd made a fool of me.

And if I'd have stayed in this city, I'd have drowned. I couldn't be that close to him.

My desperation to get away had given me the drive to convince my father to let me expand our company in Europe.

I hadn't looked back.

I learned to live with the hate that had filled the spot where my heart once lived.

Sitting here waiting for Cal proved I'd made the right decision to get as far away as I could from him.

If I hadn't, I'd have spent the past eleven years doing this very thing. Waiting for a man who didn't want me.

Why do you want him now?

Because he still made me feel protected. Even if it was false.

I needed someone to lean on. Who was I kidding? I needed him.

But this time, I knew what to expect. He couldn't blindside me again.

It was impossible for him to hurt me any worse when I'd been living with the pain since he'd so cruelly ended things.

He'd gotten what he wanted from me all those years ago. Now it was time for me to get what I wanted from him.

I just hadn't figured out what that was yet.

CHAPTER THIRTY-FOUR

CAL

"WHY DON'T you tell me who did that so I can go break his face?"

She climbed into the passenger seat and slammed the door. "Thanks for reminding me I look like a punching bag."

I growled. Her bruises had deepened in color. The makeup wasn't working.

"You need a reminder. So it doesn't happen again."

She aggressively buckled her seatbelt. "So it's my fault?"

I gripped the steering wheel and willed patience. "*No.*"

Her brows shot up. Then she tossed her purse on the floor and sat cross-legged in the seat.

Just like she used to.

She leaned her head back like it was too heavy to hold up anymore. "I didn't call you so we could argue."

"Good. Cause I didn't come pick you up to fight."

I needed her. Needed to be in her orbit, even if it was just for a little while, so she could make everything else disappear.

"Should we go to the zoo?"

Her lips twitched.

I pulled into the street and eased to a stop at the traffic light.

"I can't go chasing after you into the camel enclosure."

She lolled her head toward me. "I just wanted to feed them."

A few drops of rain hit the windshield. "Looks like Mother Nature is giving us a sign to skip the zoo."

"I'm not afraid of a little rain, but since you are, fine." She turned up the radio.

I cringed at being caught again listening to our old tapes when "Driver's Seat" by Sniff 'n' the Tears came through the speakers.

She tapped her foot to the beat. She'd always loved that song. *Wonder if she'll rewind it like she used to?*

A wander down memory lane was a dangerous path . . . one I'd been taking far too often lately.

But resisting Beau in any capacity was impossible.

Having her in the flesh was better than the deluded fantasies I'd spent the past eleven years with.

I cruised the streets at an easy pace, in no hurry with no destination in mind. I was twenty-seven again, had the girl of my dreams beside me.

Except now she didn't want me. Was stronger than me.

And there wasn't a kernel of hope that someday we'd figure out a way to be together. That maybe her father would accept me, and Teague would realize I was the right guy for his sister. And Beau would be happy, even if I couldn't afford all the things she was used to.

I could love her enough.

The rain fell harder, and I turned up the windshield wipers.

I'd done the right thing letting her go. Look at the woman she'd become. She'd conquered the world. I'd have only held her back.

But I wasn't all that sorry she didn't have a husband and kids.

Watching her move on would've sent me to an early grave.

"Did your dad push you to be a firefighter?"

I rubbed my face to clear my head. *Dangerous, dangerous thoughts.*

"Nah. I never wanted to be anything else. Not even when I was a kid."

Maybe he'd expected it of all of us, but if he had, he'd never said anything. It was in our blood.

If I wasn't a fireman, who would I be?

She fiddled with her gold chain. "My father didn't push me into real estate either."

There was a hint of surprise in her voice, like she was only just now realizing that.

She looked down. "I guess he didn't have to. I always do what he wants without him telling me to."

I hated she felt that way, as if she was a prisoner.

"Would you choose something different?"

She sniffed bitterly. "No. I love it. Love working with my brother."

I didn't bother to point out they lived on two different continents. I had no idea the dynamics of their business. Obviously, they were close, so maybe the distance wasn't a factor.

God knew it hadn't mattered to me. I couldn't stop thinking about her whether we were in the same room or a world apart.

"Why have I always been able to talk to you? It's like I can't control my mouth." She stared at me, aggravation in her posture.

"Sometimes we just need somebody to hear us."

"You don't deserve to know my thoughts."

Stab.

It was true, but I wanted them. Wanted to live inside her head because it was better than mine.

"Nobody is worthy of them."

"Yet you get my thoughts and my virginity." She looked away like she hadn't meant to say that.

I hadn't deserved that gift either and got no satisfaction she regretted giving it to me. How could she not after what I'd said?

I'd lied to her for her own good. And as much as I wanted to set her straight, I couldn't. She wouldn't believe me anyway.

She's still giving me her body.

I couldn't touch her while she was hurt. Not until she healed. It was her thoughts I craved most. She didn't need to know that either.

The song ended and she pressed rewind. In some ways it was painful because it was so familiar.

"I didn't take anything you didn't willingly give," I muttered.

"My fault again." She clutched that necklace like a lifeline.

"Do you remember her at all?" I flicked my chin toward the gold chain.

She never took it off.

"No." She dropped her chin to her chest. "Lincoln said Mom always wore it. Even when she died."

My chest tightened. Her mother had been brutally murdered, and Beau had never gotten the chance to know her. That necklace was a connection, a piece of her mom Beau refused to be without.

It had glinted in the moonlight the first time I'd seen her naked.

How could a necklace have so much history on such polar opposite ends of the spectrum? One of the best moments of my life and the worst of her mother's.

"How did you end up with it?"

She'd been too young to wear it immediately after her mom's passing. In some ways I was surprised her mother hadn't been buried with it. My father always wore a cross that had been my grandfather's. We'd put him in the ground with it on. Somehow it hadn't seemed right to separate him from the necklace.

"I found it in her jewelry box when I was five." She fisted the gold. "It's so strange. He never moved any of her things. Almost like he thought she was coming back."

"Ma keeps Dad's pocket watch on the dresser. It's been six years." That probably wasn't helpful, but it wasn't completely out of the ordinary for people to keep mementos of the people they loved close by.

These tapes were all I had left of Beau, and I refused to box them up or throw them away.

"But I mean *nothing*. Her clothes are still in their closet. Her brushes are on the bathroom counter. It's all frozen in time. This happened thirty-four years ago. I saw all of it last night, and it looks just like it did when I was a kid."

I'd give her that it was weird. But if Beau and I had lived together and—I couldn't finish the thought. I wouldn't be able to touch her things. It would be like accepting she was gone. Or throwing away her life. People did it all the time. Ma had with some of Dad's stuff. But I wouldn't be able to toss it.

Maybe I was a little off like her father.

"It doesn't make sense. If someone felt so strongly about their wife that they couldn't pack up their clothes, wouldn't you think they'd look for her murderer until they found them?" she asked before I could say anything.

"I would think so," I said carefully. "Maybe it was too hard on him."

If I were in his position, I wouldn't quit until I drew my last breath.

"It's almost like the whole thing didn't happen. I've researched and there are so few news articles, it's bizarre. Her family is old New York money. There is a ton of information about her charitable work. The story should've been more interesting than an occasional mention the day after it happened." She shifted, pulling one knee to her chest.

"Back then wasn't like now—"

"I know technology has come a long way," she snapped.

"I was going to say it was probably a lot easier to bury a story if somebody wanted to."

She jerked her head toward me. "What are you saying? That he covered up information intentionally?"

"I'm not implying anything." I lifted both hands in surrender without taking them off the steering wheel. "Why don't you ask him?"

"My father?" She looked at me incredulously. "I've begged him to tell me about her most of my life. All I get are these occasional snippets when he's using them to point out my flaws."

My dad had been the first to tell me when I screwed up, Ma right behind him, but it had always been for my own good, even if I hadn't realized it at the time. Looking back, it seemed like my mistakes hurt them more than they did me.

I couldn't imagine either of them using the other as a tool to hurt.

"What about your brothers? They were older."

"They clam up." She sighed. "I understand. It's a difficult conversation, but I just want to know *something* about my mother."

I reached over and squeezed her knee. What could I say to that? Nothing that would change anything or make it better.

"Maybe you know more than you think," I blurted.

"How? I was two when she died," she challenged.

"Just that you always wear that necklace. That's like she's with you all the time. Maybe . . ." I shrugged. I sounded stupid. "Maybe she's guiding you. Maybe you're more like her than you realize."

She blinked at me. Then she covered my hand with hers, oh so tentatively tangling her fingers with mine.

"I like you better when you don't talk much." She dropped her head back to the seat.

I snorted. "You're not the only one."

She snickered. "Are you trying to make me not hate you quite so much?"

I hate you for this.

It hurt to hear her say it, even though I already knew she did.

"No." I deserved her hate.

"You want me to hate you?" she asked like she was shocked.

"No."

She put a hand to her forehead as if I were giving her a headache. But she didn't move the hand that was twined with mine.

"I don't know what's worse. Your one-word answers or talking a lot."

"You should feel how you want to feel."

She twisted to face me. Her mouth opened and closed a couple of times. I didn't want to control her. Even if it was hard to accept, I just wanted her raw honesty. The real Beau. That was all I ever wanted.

"I'm not sure what that is anymore." She sounded defeated.

I couldn't stand that.

"You'll figure it out." I rolled to a stop, the traffic ahead at a standstill. I lifted our joined hands. "Looks to me like maybe you don't hate me quite as much as you think."

CHAPTER THIRTY-FIVE

CAL

YOU OKAY?

I erased the message I'd just pecked out. I'd been on for almost twelve hours, and Beau had been on my mind the entire time. Not that that was anything new, but when she'd been far away, I could push thoughts of her away. Manage them.

But I kept replaying the past few days in my head. How something was going on, and she trusted me enough on some level to help her escape that, but not enough to tell me the truth.

I wanted to push, to make her spill it all . . . starting with the name of the woman beater. If he wanted a punching bag, he was going to get one of his own size.

Screw it.

She hardly ever answered my texts anyway.

I punched the call button on her contact and sank on the back bumper of my truck.

It rang six times.

She's not going to answer.

I pulled the phone away from my ear.

"Cal?"

I quickly pressed it back. "Hey."

I was supposed to be the one there for her in any way she wanted me, but hearing her voice eased something in me I hadn't realized was wound tight.

"Can you hang on a sec?"

A rustling came through the line before I had a chance to answer. It was almost six. I hadn't thought about her schedule when I called. I pictured she didn't have set hours, but she might be trying to wrap things up for the day.

Something sounded like it clicked and then rubbed. Then the relative quiet turned to city noise.

"Are you still there?"

"Still here." And I wasn't just talking about this phone call. But she didn't need to know that.

Judging by the long pause, maybe she did.

Then I realized there was none of the bite to her voice I'd grown used to. Like maybe she didn't totally hate me anymore.

"Did you want something?"

Okay, so maybe it was still there. *And yeah, baby sister. I want something I'll never have.*

I dug my foot into the worn pavement. "How's your—"

"It would be a lot better if you stopped reminding me," she snapped.

"Excuse me for being concerned."

"You don't get to be concerned." Her tone was low and lethal. A reminder of exactly why she thought I didn't have the right.

"See if you can stop me." I curled my fingers around the chrome bumper so tightly I was sure my fingerprints would be left in the metal.

"It took you long enough to realize you made a mistake, but it's a decade—"

"Too late. I know."

Ever since I walked out of her life, questions had burned through me. Wanting to know if I'd done the right thing. Needing confirmation that she'd reached every goal she'd wanted to go after. That she'd been better off without me. And right now, it felt as though time was running out for some reason. Something was changing, but I didn't know what it was. And the questions lingered. Tore at me.

"Have you had a good life?" I asked quietly, glad I had something to lean on when she answered.

"Yes."

"Did you accomplish everything you wanted?"

"Mostly."

"Are you happy?" This one would be the gut punch.

"When I'm not in New York, yes. I'm happy."

"Then I didn't make a mistake."

My chest tightened to the point I could barely breathe. She'd confirmed my worst fears and greatest hope.

I was no good for her.

If she'd been shackled by me, I'd have only held her back. Without me, she'd been able to fly. To have the life she deserved.

It hurt, but I'd never be sorry for that.

"Will you meet me?" She spoke so softly I almost didn't hear her.

"I can't. Got twelve more hours on shift to go." I had the urge to blow off work. Maybe it was my ego, or maybe it was false hope, but she needed me. I *felt* it.

Getting tangled up with Beau hadn't been smart on so many levels. Just because I'd let her go didn't mean I couldn't be there for her in whatever way she needed.

My motives weren't completely unselfish. I needed any piece of her she'd give me. Even if it was only the angry ones.

"Tell me who hurt you."

I had to know. Beau could take care of herself, but I couldn't stop my need to defend her. The rage every time I thought about her bruised face and hurt arm was almost blinding.

"It's not import—"

"Someone hurting you needs to learn not to try to break precious things."

A strangled noise escaped her.

"He's not worth you getting in trouble," she whispered.

"If he doesn't touch you again, it's more than worth the trouble."

I didn't know who the bastard was to Beau. Not only would he never lay another finger on her, but I planned to make it clear he'd have to erase her from his memory. Because he wouldn't bother her again.

"Cal..."

"I want a name."

She was quiet so long I thought she'd hung up.

"Alex Davenport."

Alex Davenport.

Alex Davenport.

I couldn't wait to get my hands on him. *Should I squeeze his jaw until it broke, just like he'd done to Beau? Or should I break his arms first?*

"What are you going to do?"

I crossed my ankles. "Play checkers with him."

"Cal—"

"Don't call me that." I hated it. Then again, I didn't deserve to be special to her.

"Damn it. I have to go." It sounded like she was scrambling around. "Please don't do something stupid."

She was gone before I could answer.

Alex Davenport. Where do you live, asshole?

I opened a browser on my phone and searched his name.

What the actual hell?

Alex Davenport had landed the first blow and it was hard enough to make me see stars. I rubbed my eye but the first headline didn't change.

Engagement Announcement! Two dynasties unite. Alex Davenport and Beau Hollingsworth to wed this weekend.

CHAPTER THIRTY-SIX

BEAU

"I EXPECT IMPECCABLE BEHAVIOR."

Father hissed in my ear before he kissed my cheek.

He placed a hand on the small of my back and guided me into the parlor, where the Davenports were waiting. Once again, I felt like a show pig on display.

It was after seven and neither of my brothers were anywhere to be found. Part of me hoped they didn't show. Pretending to want to marry Alex would be much harder in front of them.

What if they bring Lexie and Pepper?

Lexie would see right through my act, and I was pretty sure Pepper would too. If Miss Adeline tagged along, it would be over. That woman wasn't afraid to call bull when she saw it.

Alex stood and beamed like I was the light of his life. Actually, it was more like he was so close to getting his hands on the prize . . . not me, but my family's power and money.

He was here and in one piece, although there hadn't been time for Cal to pay him a visit.

You should've kept your mouth shut.

It wasn't right to put Cal in that position. I had no doubt he would teach Alex a very tough lesson on how to treat women. But Cal didn't understand the rules of this world. He had no idea what the Davenports could do to him.

Lincoln and Teague could accomplish the same thing and the Davenports wouldn't give them any trouble. Because there were serious consequences. The biggest one losing this potential union.

I didn't want anything to happen to Cal. Not because of me.

I hadn't forgiven him—not even close—but he'd been there for me when I needed him. I wouldn't forget that.

Maybe he'll beat Alex to a pulp and he'll be too bruised to possibly go on with the wedding.

No. The thought was selfish.

I had no remorse over wishing Alex would feel what it was like to be scared and powerless and battered. Right or wrong, I wasn't into taking the higher road.

It was the consequences to Cal I wasn't keen on.

Why does he want to help me?

He didn't care. He'd told me so when he'd dumped me.

His words had been cruel, but his actions now said something different.

Even when things were just physical, there wasn't a distance in his touch. *Fire.* Every trail of his fingers over my body was the caress of a man who wasn't indifferent. Not of one who was just using me. No one had ever touched me the way he did.

And if I was honest, I hadn't forgotten his earlier words. When he'd asked me if I'd had a good life, accomplished what I'd wanted, was happy in London. But that final line had knocked all the breath from my lungs.

Then I didn't make a mistake.

Surely he wasn't suggesting that he let me go so I could accomplish things in life. I could have done that with him by my side. But did he think that? That he wasn't enough . . . for me.

Father nudged me in the back, an order to go to Alex. *Shouldn't he at least meet me halfway?*

Instead, I was expected to go to him like the dutiful girl I was. The woman in me rebelled.

I should've taken my old escape route off the roof while I'd been up there talking to Cal. But the thought of Lincoln and Teague destroyed over losing who they loved stopped me cold.

You can do this. For them.

"Mr. and Mrs. Davenport. Alex." I couldn't force the lie that it was lovely to see them out of my mouth. Because it was the ugliest thing I'd ever witnessed.

The doorbell rang, a powerful pong of chimes unlike an average doorbell. Because the Hollingsworth house wasn't meant to be like others.

"Late. As usual." There was a hint of pride in my father's voice I didn't understand.

Winston led my brothers into the parlor. Teague looked miserable. He hated this house as much as Lincoln and I did. Maybe more.

I was grateful to see Lexie and Pepper weren't with them.

I rushed over to them, hugging them a little too hard.

"Why does this feel like a funeral parlor?" Teague whispered.

"Because this house is a tomb," I whispered back, feeling normal for just a minute.

I couldn't remember the last time all three of us had been here together. But it was a relief. When they'd moved out and I'd been here on my own with Father for a couple years, it had been almost unbearable. They'd made living in this house more tolerable.

"Then why do you choose to stay here?" Lincoln asked.

I cut my gaze to his. He knew I didn't choose it.

"You're staying here?" Teague gaped at me in disbelief.

"Winston, the champagne, please." Father steered me toward the Davenports and beckoned my brothers over. "I believe you know my sons, Lincoln and Teague." His introduction held a note of respect that we all knew to be false.

The act of happy family had grown so tiresome.

Teague, Lincoln, and I were happy. But we were miserable around our father.

Handshakes exchanged and murmured greetings. The air was awkward and stale.

How was I going to convince my brothers I was excited about marrying Alex when I couldn't bring myself to even stand next to him?

Winston rounded the room with a silver tray of champagne flutes bubbling with the muted gold liquid. I'd always liked the color and the bubbles, though now it brought me no comfort.

Automatically, I took a glass, though I didn't sip. I was already on edge, and the thought of any food or drink made me ill.

Teague declined a glass, but like me, Lincoln took one. We were the trained animals. Teague had more courage, though Lincoln most certainly wasn't a coward. He simply had a different way of handling our father.

"To the future Mr. and Mrs. Hollingsworth." Father lifted his glass and chuckled. "I meant Davenport. I suppose I'm having a harder time letting go of my darling girl than I thought."

The Davenports joined him, the fake laughter tinkling through the room.

"It's fabulous your family has the same values as ours. So close-knit." Mrs. Davenport sipped her champagne. "This union is simply perfect."

Lincoln didn't touch his drink either. Teague appeared to be analyzing the entire situation. And Alex downed his glass in one swallow.

"Our families will do great things together," Father said, raising his glass again.

Is stealing someone else's company doing great things together?

I still hadn't figured out how I was supposed to pull that off, not that I was going to. I didn't much care for the Davenports, but I wouldn't ever try to take away what someone else had built. Or inherited, as the case may have been.

"What is it about Beau that made you realize you can't live without her?"

My lips parted. Lincoln's question was tactical, but before Lexie I didn't think he thought in terms of not being able to live without someone.

Alex would fail to answer adequately. And in a few seconds my brothers would know this whole thing was a sham. Well, their suspicions would be confirmed.

"Your sister is the most coveted woman in the city. Any man should be so lucky as to have her." Father's declaration was directed at Alex, a not-so-gentle reminder that as quickly as he gained the title of my fiancé, he could lose it.

"I couldn't agree more. But I'd like to hear from Alex."

"She's a challenge." Alex slithered his gaze to mine. "She's unlike any person I've ever known, and she certainly keeps things interesting."

On the surface, his answer actually wasn't that bad. But I understood the underlying meaning. If we started a life together, what happened in front of his parents' house was only a preview of the things to come.

He wanted to beat me into submission.

Even my father had never been that cruel.

I'd take mind games any day over bruises and near-broken bones.

Lincoln swung his attention to me. Discreetly, I shook my head, silently begging him not to ask the same question of me.

"Do you love him?"

I guessed I got what I asked for. A different question. One that was much worse.

My tongue tingled as I forced myself to keep my mouth shut. The automatic answer was easy and desperate to come out.

The lie . . . it was in my brain, but the one word refused to form.

"Where are Lexie and Pepper?" Father asked as if he were regretful they weren't with us.

He couldn't care less about their whereabouts. He'd asked for my benefit. A reminder if I didn't answer properly what that meant for my brothers.

Lincoln's brows dipped. Teague crossed his arms.

"Mr. Hollingsworth, the dining room is prepared," Winston said formally.

"Shall we have dinner?" Father portrayed the ultimate host. He pretended other people had a choice in matters when it came to him. But no one did.

Whether it was dinner or marriage, what he said went.

He ushered the Davenports out of the parlor. I remained rooted in place.

I can't sit through an entire meal pretending I'm a blushing bride-to-be. I can't.

"I don't like him," Teague said. "You're a challenge? What kind of answer is that?"

Lincoln pried the champagne flute from my fingers. "You don't have to marry him."

I snorted incredulously. "And how do you propose I avoid it?"

Damn it, Beau. You're supposed to act like this is what you want.

Lincoln squeezed his eyes shut as if in pain. "I'll take care of this."

"No," I said quickly.

Both of them looked at me with furrowed brows.

"You don't want to marry that guy." Teague pointed his thumb in the direction of the dining room. "At least have the decency not to lie to us."

"I do want to marry him." Even I didn't believe me. That was the most unconvincing declaration in the history of declarations.

"You need to get out of this house. He's—"

"Are my children going to join us for dinner? Or continue to make me look as if I'm not at the helm of this family?"

Father was a looming presence. Maybe his hand had never tightened around my throat physically, but even from across the room, it felt as if it was.

"She's not marrying him." Lincoln stood closer to me, like a shield.

"He's not even close to good enough for her." Teague flanked my other side.

"Out of anyone, I'd have expected the two of you to respect your sister's judgment." He put his hands in his pockets. "I see you're determined to keep making decisions on her behalf."

"Beau is perfectly capable of deciding what's best."

I appreciated Lincoln's confidence in me. He'd not only proven he believed that with his words, but by trusting my judgment when it came to important business deals. Ones he could've very easily taken the lead.

With my brothers on each side of me like a protective wall, it gave me a confidence that we were stronger than our father. That maybe we were in control after all.

"*You're* the one who thinks he's dictator of the world," Teague said.

"I'm the one who's looking out for Beau's best interest by securing a future for her and her offspring."

"Are you pregnant?" Teague asked incredulously.

"No," I said as if he'd lost his mind.

I shuddered at the thought of Alex touching me, let alone bearing his children.

Father smiled though it held no warmth. If anything, it chilled me to the bone.

"The two of you should be cheerleading this wedding. Do you not both want Beau back in New York?"

"Not if it isn't what you want," Teague said quietly, his focus solely on me.

Lincoln gave nothing away, but his stance had always been clear. He'd prefer I be within his watchful eyes.

"I have to say, I've been surprised she hasn't been more generous of her time with her brothers, especially if it's so limited before her return to London." Father leaned on the doorframe, cool as always. Like he was the all-knowing and we were simply pawns in his game.

Teague glared. "Maybe if you didn't work her to the bone—"

"Funny that." Father tapped his lips with his index finger. "She hasn't been at the office much. Perhaps you should ask your friend . . . oh, what *is* his name?"

My blood ran cold.

Teague and Lincoln looked at me, but I could only stare at our father.

"It's not a good precedent for a healthy marriage to sneak around, sweetheart." He had pretending to be a concerned father nailed perfectly.

"Beau, what the hell is he talking about?" Teague asked carefully.

"Ah, I remember his name now."

Father narrowed his gaze, cutting straight through me. I wanted to hold on to my brothers as my knees weakened.

"Garrett Calhoun."

CHAPTER THIRTY-SEVEN

CAL

"HOLLINGSWORTH? You lost? Or are you moving stations?"

Teague stepped into my space, his jaw locked as he glared at me. "Are you fooling around with Beau behind my back?"

Shit.

I'd dreaded this moment for a long time.

Did Beau finally tell him about us?

I glanced over his shoulder to find he wasn't alone. Lincoln was right behind him. He might have been in a suit, but he looked like he could beat my ass in about point three seconds.

Teague balled his fists. "I always wondered why she hated you. What did you do to hurt my sister?"

The station had gone silent. A few of the guys gathered to see what was going on.

"How long has this been going on?"

I stared at my friend, unsure what to say. But I wasn't mad at him. I understood. Maybe not completely since I didn't have a sister, but if I did, I sure as hell wouldn't want her with someone the likes of me.

"Answer me." His tone had gone quiet. That was almost more unnerving than his rage.

And some tiny speck of hope buried way down deep sprouted. If she'd finally told her brothers about me, what did that mean? I couldn't see the point if she wasn't going to hang around in New York more than five minutes. If she didn't want to see more of me without sneaking around.

You can't have her.

Now that we'd lost our cover, it was well and truly done. I hated myself for even thinking this could be a beginning.

I shrugged. "Nothing to say. Sorry you wasted a trip all the way over here."

I got back to checking the truck. We'd just returned from a call, and I needed to make sure everything was back in place for the next one.

"You don't think you should've asked me? What if she was your sister?"

I turned, holding his gaze. "I wouldn't let her near a bastard like me."

"I deserve to know."

"Nothing for you to know." My words were indifferent when I was anything but.

"You keep saying *nothing*. Are you saying Beau is nothing?"

I braced myself for a punch. Because the wild look on his face told me he was quickly running out of patience. The silent brother behind him looked ready to rumble too.

"No."

And that one syllable gave away that she was more to me than anything. Beau was everything. Always had been. Always would be.

He flinched. "I'm not leaving until you tell me what you did to make her hate you."

I gestured toward a chair by the wall. "Take a load off. Cause you're gonna be here a while."

"You're like a brother to me. We went through the academy together."

I couldn't stand that he thought I'd betrayed his trust. But I had. At first, when Beau and I had started sneaking around, there wasn't a reason to tell him. I wasn't going to ask permission to see his sister. Hell, maybe that would've been the right thing to do.

The longer things went on, the harder it was to tell Teague.

And Beau didn't want to.

What she wanted was more important to me.

Then we were done, and she moved to another country.

I didn't see a reason to potentially lose a friend when my relationship with Beau was in the past.

I folded my arms and leaned against the fire truck. "I saw in the paper she's getting married. Shouldn't you be grilling that guy instead of me?"

"You don't read the paper," Teague said. "And I'll deal with him too."

It's him you should be concerned about, buddy. He's given you a real reason to fight.

And I probably should mention what that bastard had done to Beau. Because if Teague knew, he wouldn't be here with me right now.

But it was my place to protect her.

I couldn't stand the thought of her married, especially to someone like him. And as soon as I got off work, Alex Davenport and I were going to have a little chat.

"Hollingsworth, are you disrupting my station?" Captain Dunn emerged from his office, looking pissed.

"Just need a word with Cal."

"Do it on his off time. The department doesn't pay him to socialize." He turned on his heel and went out back, undoubtedly to smoke since he had a two pack a day habit.

"I can't get suspended, man," I said.

Teague's face hardened and he pointed at me. "You're going to have a lot more to worry about than that when I get the truth." He jerked his head toward the door. "Let's get out of here."

His brother gave me a long, menacing stare before following him toward the back door. Somehow that was more intimidating than a verbal threat.

Teague turned around and walked backward. "Stay away from my sister."

Not until she tells me she's done.

Stab.

That thought hurt worse than any punch Teague could land.

There had always been an expiration date on whatever it was Beau and I were doing. Suddenly, it felt like it just got a lot closer.

"You dog." Brennan slapped my shoulder. "Hollingsworth's sister? Damn, man. She's the hottest chick I've ever seen."

I'd kept my temper in check the entire time Teague and Lincoln were here, mostly because they were right to be mad. But it skyrocketed when Brennan talked about Beau like that. Like she was an object.

"Watch your mouth."

He stepped back and held up his hands. "I wondered if Hollingsworth had it wrong; you played it so cool with him. If he'd seen that reaction, he'd know you've most definitely been sneaking around with her."

"I don't blame you, dude." Vigiano gave me a *right on* gesture. "An ass beating from Hollingsworth would be worth it for her."

Scopetta punched his shoulder and laughed. "Hollingsworth would knock out Cal in one punch."

"My money's on Hollingsworth too." Brennan pulled out a ten-dollar bill and waved it.

They all placed bets like it would be the rumble of the century.

"You're all idiots," I grumbled. "I'm not fighting Hollingsworth."

"You might not have a choice."

"There are ways to settle things like men," I said. Except with Alex Davenport. He'd put his hands on Beau. And he was going to feel my hands on him.

Captain came back in, a cloud of smoke following him. He pulled me aside. "You better go, Cal. PD just hauled in your brother."

Damn it, Joe. What have you done now?

I just prayed no one was hurt this time.

"He at the station down the street?"

"Yeah." Captain lowered his voice. "I'll clock you out when your shift's over."

I wanted to hug the man. "Thanks."

"Bobby would have my ass if I didn't."

I nodded. "Do you know if it's another DUI?" I dug my keys out of my pocket.

"Not DUI. Arson."

CHAPTER THIRTY-EIGHT
BEAU

"MY DEAR, dear daughter. Have you forgotten the consequences of your behavior?"

I sat stiffly in the chair across from Father's desk in his study. Lincoln and Teague hadn't stayed for dinner. Teague had been on a warpath when he'd stormed out of the house. Lincoln had been right behind him.

I didn't mean for you to find out that way. I didn't mean for you to find out at all.

Our father was strategic. He hated the sight of his children in a united front. So he did what any general would against his enemy. He divided us.

And I felt that chasm between my brothers and me acutely.

"No," I finally answered.

Dinner with the Davenports had been filled with Mr. and Mrs. Davenport chattering on about nothing as if my brothers hadn't ever been there. I'd always found it odd how people in my father's world were masters at keeping the outer shell looking perfect. No blips, no bumps in the road, never ruffled. But inside the walls was drama and chaos and imperfection they'd never allow anyone else to see.

Father, too, had behaved as if Lincoln and Teague didn't exist.

I had pushed food around my plate for two hours and hadn't bothered to put up the pretense of listening. Alex had courted my father as if *he* were the one he needed to impress. Not me.

"I thought you would've cut off your relationship with that common man given you're betrothed to another." He opened the filing drawer in his desk. "Whether or not you're faithful to your husband is irrelevant to me, except if I can catch you, so can anyone else. That is unacceptable."

You'll never stop your frightening stalking, will you?

Somewhere in the back of my head, I thought I was pulling off seeing Cal without him knowing. It was foolish thinking.

There was nothing that escaped Samuel Hollingsworth. And even then, Cal had tried to protect me. To lose my father's tail when he'd followed us.

"When you were gallivanting with him before, I'd hoped you'd come to your own realization that he wasn't good enough for you." He sighed, pulled out a folder, and closed the drawer. "Your judgment can't be trusted."

He opened the file and scanned through a few documents.

"Not only was your relationship with him a disgrace to this family . . ." He looked at me with a steely gaze. "Which you knew, otherwise you wouldn't have kept it from your brothers."

No. My relationship with Cal hadn't been a disgrace to my family. I was young and stupid and scared of my brother for no reason at all. Looking back, it was absurd. But the secret had become easier to keep than telling the truth. It still amazed me that we dated for as long as we did without Teague finding out.

Seeing how it ended, though, how I was duped by Cal, maybe my instinct had been right.

And maybe my father was right that Cal wasn't the man for me . . . it was his reasoning that was so very wrong.

"I've been too lenient." He tapped the papers. "You've made a fool of me. I thought the issue was resolved when you ran off to London."

My palms grew damp. I'd begged and pleaded with Father to let me go, desperate to get away from Cal and all the heartbreak.

"I felt the distance was best back then, so I allowed you to go."

I was a puppet, who thought she'd had a choice.

"Since it's quite clear time and distance and experience has not made you wiser, you leave me no choice." He pressed his lips together as if in deep contemplation. "The thing about people like that Calhoun rodent is that there are so many ways to get a point across. It's almost unfair they make so many poor choices. I have a buffet of options to make it clear he isn't to see you again."

Even at the point I hated Cal the most, I never would've wished my father's wrath on him. Never.

And I didn't now.

"Since you're so *intimate* with him." He paused to let the implication sink in. "What do you think would be the most effective? His mother, his brother, or his massive debt?"

Contempt. That was what I felt toward my father.

How could he hurt innocent people? What would he do to them? And Cal was in debt?

"I won't see him again."

His face was as hard as I'd ever seen it. "Oh, I know you won't. But it's too late. You both need to understand that the tryst is over."

"Please, don't—"

"And whatever I decide, you can remember that *you* brought this upon them."

Guilt hit me swiftly, nearly taking me under.

I had to warn Cal. He might not know what my father's wrath would bring, but at least he and his family wouldn't be blindsided by it. Father would do something to Cal's mom? One of his brothers? But hadn't they suffered enough already? Losing Cal's dad?

What was wrong with the monster in front of me?

He closed the folder. "Try to concentrate on what's important. Which is getting the Davenport's company."

With a chin flick, I was dismissed.

Inside, I shook with desperation and regret. I had to get to Cal.

"And sweetheart, you're far too old to be escaping off the roof."

I was a prisoner.

Nothing was my own. And because *Father* didn't like when I strayed, other people were going to pay the consequences. Which he knew would be far more painful and effective than anything he could do to me.

I changed into jeans, a sweater, and flats and rushed toward the window. I *was* too old to be doing this, but I had no other choice.

I yanked, and it wouldn't budge. I checked the latches, which were open, and tried again.

Nothing.

And then I saw it. The board on the outside preventing the window from opening.

Only a few hours ago I'd been out there.

Any hope I had of avoiding this marriage was squashed out.

But I had to try to warn Cal and pray that it didn't cost him even more.

Because any smart prisoner always had more than one escape route.

CHAPTER THIRTY-NINE

CAL

"MY JOE DIDN'T BURN down that house."

Ma tore her apron off and threw it on the counter.

I appreciated her adamant belief in my brother's innocence. No matter how hard things got, she was there to support us.

"We'll find a lawyer to help him," I said.

I'd come straight to Ma's after stopping by the jail to check on Joe. He'd refused to see me.

And I'd had to be the one to deliver the bad news to Ma.

I pulled her in for a hug.

She clung to me tightly. "I'm going to call that Jack Petty. We went to high school together. He needs to release Joe immediately."

"I've already talked to him." Bobby trudged into the kitchen. "Nothing he can do right now."

"He's the chief. If anybody can do something it should be him." Ma wrestled out of my hold and went to the refrigerator. "Sit. I'll fix something to eat."

I didn't want any food. It was almost midnight, and what I really needed was one night of peace.

But cooking for her boys was what made Ma happy, so I'd eat for her.

Bobby tossed his keys on the counter. "Any word on when he's getting out?"

Aaron was right behind him. "Who they really need to look at is that crazy Christina."

The woman had lost her mind. A few days ago, I'd have said no way, but after the way she'd acted lately . . . I agreed with my brother.

"If it's arson, insurance won't pay." Mike filed in behind my other brothers. "You know he refinanced that thing less than a year ago to pay for those fertility treatments."

Yeah, I knew. Because I'd been helping him make the payments.

"He didn't do it!" Ma threw a wooden spoon on the counter and pushed her way through the wall of sons out of the kitchen.

"I'll go check on her," Mike said.

A silence descended on the kitchen. We'd had a lot of good times in this very spot and a lot of bad ones too.

It didn't look good for Joe, but we'd figure out a way to pull through as a family.

That was what we did.

"I talked to the inspector." Bobby sat down at the table. "Joe's in trouble."

If I told anyone what he'd said to me the night we'd gone over to get some of his things, he'd be in even more trouble.

My phone rang, but I made no move to pull it from my pocket.

"Aren't you gonna answer?" Aaron pointed at me. "It could be something about Joe."

I stood and slipped it out.

"I'll be back." I held up the phone to my brothers.

It stopped ringing, but I called the number back as I tracked through the living room to the front door.

"I have to see you." Beau sounded desperate as her voice barreled into my ear.

She rarely called.

Every one of my senses went on high alert. I closed the front door behind me and paced on the stoop.

"He touch you again?"

"No. Please, Cal. Where are you? I'll meet you."

This was different than the night she'd been hurt. Fear was in every syllable.

My family needed me, but so did Beau.

"I'll come pick you up."

"East 92nd and Park."

The front door opened and Bobby stuck his head out. "That news about Joe?"

I shook my head. "I'll be there soon." I hung up and pocketed my phone again. "I gotta run. Call me if anything happens."

"Cal, we're in a crisis here." He threw his hands up.

"I know, and I'll be back as soon as I can."

I jogged to my truck and fired it up.

I'm coming, baby sister. I'm coming.

CHAPTER FORTY

BEAU

CAL'S TRUCK.

Relief rushed through me at the sight of it. He'd made it quickly, though it felt like an eternity.

The passenger door opened as he rolled to a stop and I climbed inside.

It was like we'd never stopped doing this.

"I'm sorry," I blurted the second I shut the door.

"For what?" he asked carefully.

"Stupid. Stupid. Stupid." I covered my face with my hand, ignoring the pain in my arm at the sudden movement.

How could I have put him in this position? Especially after he'd been there for me when I needed someone most?

"Teague isn't gonna beat my ass." Gently, he pulled my hand away from my face.

"Teague?"

Oh no. In all my haste, I'd forgotten about my brothers.

"He and Lincoln paid me a visit at the station." He changed lanes. "I gotta say, I'm pretty shocked you told them about us."

"And they threatened to beat you up?"

Denying that I'd told them should've been the first thing out of my mouth. My brothers were overprotective, but I didn't really think they'd hurt Cal . . . at least I'd hoped they wouldn't.

"Nah. They flexed a little muscle, but that's it."

"What did you tell them?" My stomach somersaulted.

"Nothing."

"Nothing?"

"I figured you'd told them what you wanted them to know, so it wasn't my place to divulge anything more." He turned onto the next street. "Are you really going to marry that asshole?"

I blinked at him. How did Cal know about that?

"I have to." I squeezed my eyes closed. "But I can't."

"You don't have to do anything." He said it so easily, as if telling them all to take a hike was no big deal.

"My father is going to hurt you or your family. I don't know how, but he's doing it to make sure I do what he wants. I'm sorry, Cal. I'm so, so sorry."

That guilt rushed back with a vengeance. I'd been selfish, trying to do what Father wanted and what I wanted too. It didn't work that way. Only my father's wishes were important. Everything else be damned.

"When you say hurt . . . what do you mean?"

I swallowed hard. "He said he hadn't decided if it would be your mother, your brother, or you. He knows you're in debt." I twisted in my seat. "Are you in debt?"

My father danced between the line separating truth and lies. Maybe he'd embellished to get my attention.

"What's he gonna do to my ma or my brothers?" he asked through his teeth.

"I-I don't know. Whatever it is, we can't stop it. I just thought I should warn you."

He drummed the steering wheel and stared straight ahead.

"I never meant to drag you into this mess," I whispered.

"I'm in it now, aren't I?"

I touched his thigh, and he jerked as if it was painful.

"If I promise to marry Alex, maybe that will help. Maybe he won't hurt any of you," I said almost to myself. It wasn't just Cal's family at risk, it was my brothers too.

The weight of it all pressed so heavily on my shoulders, I thought it would break me.

"And what good is that if that bastard kills you? Because that's what's coming. You know that, right?" Cal's voice was so tight and fierce, it cut through me.

I did know.

And I didn't want to end up dead for Alex Davenport or my father.

But for my brothers and Cal, I'd do anything.

I recoiled. The thought had come too easily.

I looked at the man across the cab of the truck. He was the only one I'd ever loved. The person I'd hated most. He'd ruined me for all others.

But it was true. I would do anything to protect him from my father.

What if *I* was the shield he needed?

I'd never tested my father's limits. And he'd certainly wielded threats against me and my brothers, but had they ever amounted to much more than that?

They were scare tactics to get us to fall in line. And most of the time we did because we were afraid he would follow through on his threats.

At some point, I had to be brave and test those limits. Otherwise, I'd never be free.

Neither would Teague, Lincoln, or Cal.

I brought my phone screen to life and did a quick search. In a minute, I had the information I needed.

"Drive to Connecticut."

"What the hell do you want to go there for?"

I gripped my phone and prayed this was the answer. "I have to try to outsmart him. This has to stop."

"You are smarter than that ass. But how many bruises is it going to take—"

"Not Alex. My father." I squeezed his thigh. "I need your help."

I'd asked a lot of Cal lately. And if I could come up with any other way, I would. But this could protect us all.

He looked down at where I touched him before lifting his gaze to mine. "How am I supposed to do that?"

I sucked in a deep breath. Everything hinged in the balance. But if I kept doing the same thing, we'd all suffer.

"Will you marry me?"

ENJOY THIS BOOK?

You can make a huge difference.

Reviews encourage other readers to try out a book. They are critically important to getting your favorite books in the hands of new readers.

We'd appreciate your help in spreading the word. If you could take a quick moment to leave a review on your favorite book site, we would be forever grateful. It can be as short as you like. You can do that on your favorite book retailer, Goodreads, and BookBub.

Email us (grahame@grahameclaire.com) a link to your review so we can be sure to thank you. Together, we can ensure our friends aren't left out.

Thank you so very much.

ALSO BY GRAHAME CLAIRE

SHAKEN SERIES

Crash & Burn Duet

Crash

Burn

Rise & Fall Duet

Rise

Fall

Bend & Break Duet

Bend

Break

SHATTERED SERIES

Shattered Secrets

Shattered Sins

Shattered Lies

ABOUT THE AUTHOR

Grahame Claire is a *USA Today* bestselling author of contemporary romance.

    A writer. A blogger. United by our love of stories and all things romance. There was definitely some insta-love. Hello? Books involved. A little courting. A lot of writing. The result . . . Grahame Claire.

    Soulmates. Unashamed of our multiple book boyfriends. Especially the ones that rooted in our heads and wouldn't leave us alone. Don't worry. We'll share.

    Pleased to meet you.

    Our favorite thing about being an author is you, the reader. So please, reach out. If you want to get on the exclusive mailing list (trust us, you do), you can do that at www.grahameclaire.com/newsletter.

    Let's chat books on Goodreads. We can gossip about our book boyfriends on Twitter at @grahamewrites, Facebook at www.facebook.com/grahamewrites, our Facebook group Grahame Claire Reader Hangout at www.facebook.com/groups/GrahameClaireReaderHangout, Instagram @grahameclaire, or send us an email anytime at grahame@grahameclaire.com.

    Follow us on BookBub at www.bookbub.com/authors/grahame-claire

Printed in Great Britain
by Amazon